CW00862662

THE HOUSE ON BLACKSTONE HILL

ANTONIO RICARDO SCOZZE

This book is dedicated to my Nameless Ones; you know who you are.

[1]

YOU HAVE BEEN LIED TO ABOUT YOUR VERY EXISTENCE.

You have been lied to your entire life. Not just your life, but the lives of your parents, your grandparents, great-grandparents, all the way back for hundreds of generations. You and everyone you know have been lied to, and everything you think is sure in the world, every piece of firm ground upon which you have built your understanding of reality is nothing but shifting sands.

The world you *think* you live in, the world you assume to be so predictable and obvious, so mundane and average, is nothing but a thin veneer covering a much deeper, darker, dangerous world. The world you think you live in is a lie.

By and large, this lie was not perpetrated upon you and your forebearers deliberately. As time went on, the knowledge of things once well-known were forgotten, and then the memory of those things became mere myth and legend. Things became shrouded in the mist, and as so often happens, were lost. You will note, however, my Dear Friend, that I said this was *by and large* not deliberate. There were, and remain still today, cabals of very powerful, very

1

influential, and very evil people across the world who realized it was to their benefit to allow these dark, dangerous things to remain shrouded by the mists and to keep you blinded by these lies.

But these people will be exposed as time goes on and my writings unfold. Of that you may be sure, Dear Friend.

You no doubt are now wondering what are the terrible details of this great and dreadful secret? What is this huge lie that has been foisted upon you, that has made your entire life nothing but a foolish charade? What is this dark and dangerous world to which I refer?

It is this: There is an entire world of horror, a whole universe of terror, that exists with, is entwined around, and yet is just under the surface of your normal, quotidian existence. It is a perverse world that, warped as it may be, has its own internal logic, its own mores, norms, and values. This is an evil, twisted world ruled by innumerable demons from the depths of hell, bent on the torment and torture of every human being. Things you thought were mere children's tales, fanciful myths and legends, or superstitious folklore are true.

True, and horrifyingly real.

These very real things are utterly dark and perversely evil. Your worst nightmares can't possibly come close to the horrors that prowl about in the darkest corners of the world and of the human soul, looking for ways to create unending anguish and suffering, death, and destruction. The most horrible acts that humans have ever committed against each other can never compare to the horror this world delights in creating. You cannot imagine evil of this level, you are incapable of cognizing it, your mind simply cannot grasp malevolence and wickedness of this level; there is scarcely even language adequate to describe it. It is almost a language unto itself.

To know the terror that slithers around your carefully

constructed life may drive you insane with an overabundance of knowledge, so if you want to turn away now, if you'd rather live a life of blissful ignorance cradled in the lap of obliviousness, then perhaps that'd be best. Yet, if you're one of the very brave few who thirst for knowledge and want to know the truth above all else, read every word of what I have to say very carefully, my Dear Friend.

This world of which I speak is one ruled over by legions of demons, evil fallen angels tormented by their Satanic master to a hatred that has become madness. Their only wish is to inflict unending misery on humanity, whom they hold responsible for the fall. They use as many different fell tools in this torture as possible, so it is also a world in which monsters, evil spirits, and nightmarish creatures beyond counting are all horribly true. These vile creatures lurk in the deep, dark shadows of the world, creatures used to horrify, plague, or simply slaughter as many humans as possible.

It is a world of devils, too, but please note, Dear Friend, that demons and devils are not at all the same things. Demons are fallen angels, imbued with massive supernatural powers, whereas devils are twisted little creatures the demons themselves have made to further their goals, having taken them from creation. Demons cannot create any new life, they can only pervert what already exists and use it for their own evil purposes. This is what devils are, horrific beasts twisted and turned by the wicked power of a demon into a supernatural, nearly immortal monster, ever bent on death and destruction. No two devils are alike and come in as many different shapes and sizes as the twisted imagination of their masters can conceive.

Ghosts are true, too, and are used to terrorize people, to cause as much psychic angst as possible for the tortured delight of some wretched demon. These are the souls of very evil people whom the lords of hell believed would be even more tormented by being bound to a place they loved in a material world they can no longer interact with. Sometimes these spirits will be released from hell for a time to specifically torture a surviving loved one. And sometimes these are the spirits of otherwise innocent people killed in a place so powerfully demonic they cannot escape, causing that innocent soul endless anguish. I have more, much more, to write about ghosts, but this will suffice for now.

Vampires and werewolves are also very real, and for as horrifically terrifying as they are normally portrayed to be in modern culture, they are far more so in real life. More on them later as well.

Witches and wizards? Yes, they also exist, but perhaps not as you expect. Magic can only be used by gaining that power directly from a demon, so there are no good witches and wizards. They are certainly not cute little children going to quaint castles to learn these skills. These are evil, perverted people who have cruelly sacrificed the lives of many cute little children to gain these powers, which they use for their own evil purposes.

Succubi? Incubi? Ghouls? Yes, they're all real. All of them. These are all demons with their own specialized ways in which they torture and torment humans.

Zombies? Zombies are real, too, but don't get too impressed by that. A corpse can only become re-animated by a demon or a magic-user, and they are mindless tools used for the most mundane of tasks. They also have one specific weakness: They're rotting flesh. The magic that reanimates a corpse does nothing to prevent normal putrefaction, so eventually, they will literally fall to pieces. That, and they tend to freeze in the winter and attract predators in the summer, so all in all zombies are not nearly as amazing as modern culture would suggest. Nonetheless, they serve their purpose.

Mummies? Yes, of course, mummies are real. When animated they're just well-dressed zombies.

Aliens? No. Aliens don't exist. We are painfully alone in the universe. However, there are terrors that exist in the deep reaches of space, terrors that if you were to see would drive you instantly mad. Your throat would turn raw from your screams and you would shred your face bloody trying to claw out your eyes to make the terror end. We will talk more about these, later.

Perhaps the most terrifying creature of all turns out to be the demonically dedicated, Satanic worshipping human.

Truly, deeply evil people are simply a fact, and while you are by now accustomed to the idea in the modern world of violent gang members or homicidal dictators, you may not realize so much of what appears random acts of violence is in fact deliberately directed from afar – or, actually, from below. Across the world there are small covens of witches and wizards that worship Satan, drawing on him for their power, who have committed unthinkable acts of horror in furtherance of their magic. There are also individual worshippers scattered everywhere ready to do his will and who worship him through acts of serial rape and murder. These people work very hard to create a thin veneer of normalcy so that no one would ever think they bowed down to the Evil One himself.

Yet perhaps even more terrifying than these are the large numbers of people in positions of power – in governments across the world, in all the media, in universities, in the military, everywhere – dedicated to this evil, who work hand in hand with the demonic forces for the end of all things. It may horrify you to realize how organized this evil truly is. It is these people who for hundreds of years have manipulated governments, started wars and revolutions, encouraged genocide, all in name of furthering their Satanic master. It is these people, more even than the covens and the lone wolves, who are the most dangerous of all demonic followers.

And what of me, Dear Friend? What of your humble storyteller, this writer with the strange name of Antonio Ricardo Scozze? Surely by now you are wondering how I have all this dreadful knowledge, how is it I am trusted with these dark secrets, how do I come to possess this clandestine information? Ah, yes. I tell you in deepest truth, the way I come to this knowledge is a story that is both great and terrifying, terrific and appalling in and of itself. That will be a tale that unfolds slowly through my various stories, in many of which I am personally involved.

But this is a tale for a much later time. For now, let us turn our attention to a man in his office, contemplating his career...

[2]

ADAM LONG SAT IN THE BOSTON OFFICE OF THE CABLE news network where he worked, staring unhappily at the subject line of an unopened email from his general manager. *Epstein?* was all it said, but that was all he needed to see to already know what the content of the message would be.

He leaned back in his chair, his soy latte now growing cold and totally forgotten about, a foot on the opened lower drawer of his desk as was his habit. It was also his habit to cross his arms across his chest and to hold his chin in his hand when nervous or confronted with a vexing problem, which is how he now sat.

Well, fuck he thought. *She found out. This could be bad. Very bad.*

Adam glanced around his office as he thought about this, looking at the various pictures and awards he'd won over the years in his journalism career. He sighed heavily once, rubbing his chin, and thought *How did it come to this?*

An early 90s graduate of Berkley's graduate school of journalism, writing is the only thing Adam ever really wanted to do and focused on political reporting due largely to his parents' passionate involvement in a variety of southern-California political organizations. He looked at the picture of his graduation from Berkley, flanked by his parents, both of whom hold their fists high in mute defiance. His mother wore a free-flowing, bohemian dress with a garish turquoise necklace and bracelets, while his father wore a political tee-shirt, jeans, and sandals. He smiled thinking of the daily political tirades his spectacled and frizzy-haired mother would regale him with.

How could it be any other way? he thought, chuckling to himself, but his mirth was short-lived.

He thought about the long road that had taken him inevitably to this point. Adam wrote for the Sacramento paper for two years before finally getting a spot at the *Washington Post*, something he at that time thought was a dream posting. His eye glanced quickly, almost guiltily, at the picture of him beaming with both the Clintons as their time in the White House came to an end. He then looked to the one of him proudly next to Nancy Pelosi when she first became speaker, another with Chuck Schumer, and finally his favorite, the one with Obama. He was proud of the work he'd done, of the quality journalism he had contributed over the years, as well as the small and subtle ways he was able to help contribute to their, and others, political victories. Adam was perfectly comfortable using his reporting to influence important causes he believed were worth fighting for and proud to have helped forward these causes.

Why shouldn't I be proud? he thought angrily, taking in the course of his career. *Why should one damn decision ruin all this?*

His eyes lingered for a moment over the various awards he had won during his career. On his bookcase was the statuette he'd won from the GLAAD Media Awards, and on his wall his James Foley Medill medal, his SPJ New American medallion, and the framed letter he'd received announcing his earning the Hillman Prize. He'd earned all these because of his writing, of his reporting, of his decision-making skills – which included sometimes what *not* to report for the right reasons.

So why the fuck should that decision come back on me now?!

It was during the 90s that his reputation as an excellent political reporter grew and his connections in Washington deepened, so much so that it seemed he knew what was going to happen in Congress long before most representatives did. He was proud, too, of the fact that he could call elected officials and was on a first-name basis with them, would regularly be invited the lunch to offer his opinion of various points, and was trusted with information not all journalists were.

By the decade's end, these deep political connections allowed him to be recruited away from the *Post* to a position he considered even better, *The New York Times*. As far as Adam was concerned it was the very best situation possible: He could continue to live in Washington and cover politics, yet his words would now be published in a much larger and more respected paper.

The greater the vehicle, the greater the number of his readers. The larger his audience, the larger his influence. Adam liked that.

He stood now, walking to his office window so he could look out at Boston on this cold and rainy mid-November day. He stood arms akimbo, hands on his lean waist, looking out the large window on this iron-gray cloudy day. With dark mists hanging low, the skies matched his mood perfectly.

He recalled it was on a day much like this in the early 2000s that his already impressive career took a wonderfully radical new turn, one that would eventually lead him into the powerful news director position he now occupied. He recalled the day that his book was first published, a book

ANTONIO RICARDO SCOZZE

about the alleged political connections of the entire Bush family and the political maleficence of the then-current Bush president, as well as the ways in which these various threads were woven together to inevitably lead to 9/11 and to pave the way for the Iraq War. The book sold well, making him fairly wealthy, but more importantly made Adam something of a celebrity within his profession and, of greater personal significance to him, within his niche of political reporters.

Sitting back down at this desk, his arms again crossed against his chest and his clean-shaven chin nestled in his hand, he reflected how that book launched him in a wildly unexpected direction. Adam's paradigm about how to report the news had always been somewhat ossified in the era he'd grown up in, so when he thought of reporting it was always as a reporter – or editor, as he worked his way up the ranks – in a newspaper. He was not prepared for the eclipse of newspaper by digital media, but when he was offered to be the executive editor for a digital news web site called *A New Day*, he eagerly seized the new medium with both hands. Adam quickly realized the great reach and potential digital media had when combined with the nascent smartphones and their ubiquitous apps and knew his influence on political decision-making could grow exponentially.

He rubbed his high forehead as a headache started to develop there and ran his hands through his receding hair. What once was a thick mane of curly straw-colored hair had slowly crept further and further up his forehead, then thinned out considerably, due in part to the pressures of being involved in such a new, untested news reporting medium. Yet despite the pressure of not only entering a new process but also building all the upper floors as it grew, Adam relished the chance he'd had to influence the policymakers in Washington.

It was in this capacity that he'd made the decision that led to this still unopened email. Although the choice he made was long before he was recruited by the news network to be the all-powerful news director, long before he uprooted his life and family to move to Boston, Adam knew that decision would eventually be trouble here in his current job.

With a digital format, the way in which news is reported is very different than in a traditional setting, either newsprint or television. One important way this is so is there are far fewer paid reporters on staff at *A New Day*, many stories being written by reporters they would commission for a specific job, or from reporters coming with a fully developed story ready for publication. Adam had read many such articles, considered them carefully, and either made the decision to publish them or not. Though an editor in the digital outlet and no longer a political reporter, one thing he always considered in this process was the degree to which it would further the good causes for which he'd been fighting all these years.

And so it was that all the way back in 2014 a young investigative reporter presented to Adam a story alleging that a wealthy New York financier named Jeffery Epstein was not only sexually involved with minors but that he was in fact trafficking underage girls for the use of powerful people from all across the world. What made this story so salacious and shocking, and so, therefore, news-worthy was that some of the people who were allegedly raping these sex-trafficked underage girls were also some of the most powerful politicians in America.

Adam reviewed this story carefully and with trepidation. As he reviewed it again and again, he thought over the story's details with a growing sense of foreboding.

He'd heard about Epstein before. He recalled at that time reading a story in *Vanity Fair* about him all the way back in 2003, although the allegations of sex trafficking had been conveniently overlooked in that article. Wanting to know more about this well-connected and mysterious financier, he'd reached out to some of his political contacts in Washington. Since no one in Washington is capable of keeping a secret, it was well known Epstein had regular sex parties with the Washington elite, and that many of the women at these parties were young – no one seemed willing, or able, to say *how* young, but everyone agreed that they were very young.

As he learned more about the sordid details, it became clear to Adam that this story was a potential bomb waiting to go off. Though the details seemed very well-investigated and the sources thoroughly vetted, Adam feared the potential legal consequences of publishing something like this about a private citizen without anything more tangible than several young women's accusations. He also knew many of the victims came from poor households and feared it would look like nothing but a well-executed hit job on an immensely wealthy man simply for money. Adam didn't want *A New Day*'s name associated with a potential shakedown.

But of far greater concern to Adam was the fact that by publishing this story he'd be putting the political careers of some of his favorite people, some of the most powerful and influential politicians, the people he believed in, at great risk.

After nearly two weeks of deliberation, Adam found himself weighing what was for the greater good, and he decided that would be served by quashing the story. However, rather than merely declining the story as he'd done with numerous other stories, he paid the reporter for her story and had her sign an agreement legally restraining her from discussing the details of her story with anyone outside his news organization until after publication.

A publication, of course, that would never happen.

At the time Adam felt good about what he'd done, congratulating himself on making a very difficult decision. He kept the story locked in his desk, mentioned it no one, and would never return the reporter's calls asking when the story might be published. In time her calls become more and more infrequent, and when they finally stopped altogether, he was able to forget the story.

Until 2019, that is, when once again Epstein and his connections to the political elite of Washington were in the spotlight. Stories of his arrest and connections to various powerful elites were quickly followed by allegations that this story was well known among various media outlets, ones that simply chose to not publish or pursue it. When these claims against media outlets were made public by various reporters, Adam knew it was only a matter of time before his name was dredged up in this sordid mess.

Which is why, as Adam finally opened the email to read it, he confirmed he was right about its content. His general manager wanted to know if there were any truth to the accusations being made that he was aware of Epstein as early as 2014 and that he chose to quash the story. The tone of the email, he noted, was not at all confrontational, almost as if the general manager had heard nasty rumors she didn't believe and, just for the sake of due diligence, wanted to check in with Adam first. That buoyed his spirits. Perhaps he could move beyond this annoyance and focus again on doing his good work.

He decided to tread a very careful line as he mostly told his general manager the truth, but either left out or embellished a few small details. Yes, it was absolutely true the story came to his attention in 2014, and yes, the decision was made to quash the story. However, it was not so much his decision as it was the higher managerial echelons at *A New Day* that made the choice to spike it, and he was merely the guy who had to execute the order.

Adam was just about to begin writing back to his general

manager to explain what had happened when there two quick knocks on his office door and his executive producer, Teresa Sanchez, walked in, a steaming cup of coffee in hand. They met at least once every day to discuss which stories to pursue further, how to develop them, which producers should manage which stories, and all the other many things that were required to make a television news network actually work.

After about an hour of talking and planning they were done, and Teresa was just about ready to leave when she said suddenly, "Oh!"

Adam's bright blue eyes, already normally larger and pop-eyed than the average person's – he always had the look of perpetual wonder or surprise about him, something he thought as a political reporter was not necessarily a bad thing – grew now much wider. "What? What is it?"

"Do you remember the story on Cromwell's Ferry we talked about a few months ago, how there's a mist there that doesn't seem connected to the mine fire? How we thought that'd make for a good story because maybe there was something damaging to the environment going on?"

"Yeah, I recall. What about it?"

"Well, boss, turns out there's no reason anyone can find for the mist to be there, and it doesn't seem connected to the fire at all. Nothing damaging the environment, either. The reporter, Katie, spoke to all the scientists at MIT and BC and Harvard we could find, and not a one of them found anything untoward."

"Huh...OK." His wide-open, owl-like eyes seemed to say *And...?*

"Bottom line, not much of a story. Interesting, maybe do a small piece just for the web site, but not much more than that. But the thing is, Katie says Cromwell's Ferry is a pretty neat if a little spooky place. You'd said you were looking for little days trips to do with Ava and the kids. Thought you might like it. I bet Junior would get a kick out of the place."

"Yeah, I bet he would," he said with a smile. "What six-year-old boy wouldn't get a kick out of a ghost town on top of a giant underground coal fire?"

"Exactly my point. She did say the whole place stunk like a coal fire, but that's to be expected."

"Oh, wait" he said. "Is it safe for the kids? I wouldn't want them to get sick or anything."

"Of course, it is. There is carbon dioxide, but if no one sticks their face in a fire vent everything should be fine. Like I said, none of the eggheads were able to find anything overly dangerous in the air, and really the worst thing there is the smell of sulfur. People go there all the time, no biggie."

Teresa left, and Adam again applied himself to answering the email. He felt his irritation subdue from earlier, but his sense of indignation remained. *I did what I did, and I did it for a good reason*, he thought. *It's a shame some kids got hurt, it's a tragedy some sacrifices had to be made, but there are bigger things at stake here. People need to understand that.*

He wrapped up the email, and again leaned back into his chair, arms across chest, foot on drawer, hand on chin. He thought for a moment, but then his thoughts turned towards his own children and this possible day trip.

"Cromwell's Ferry, eh?" he muttered to no one in particular. "Could be fun."

[3]

THE NEXT WEEKEND, ADAM, HIS WIFE, AVA, AND THEIR two small children left their Chestnut Hill home, piled into the family Subaru, and pulled out for the two-hour drive to Cromwell's Ferry. They left the Boston area on a sunny, crisp, and cool November day, where the chill air felt fresh and invigorating. Although the countryside outside of the city had lost the autumn brilliance of just a few weeks earlier, the somber tones of the winter denuded woods and the brilliant gold fields of dried corn against the blue sky still made the drive westward gorgeous.

Adam was quite right in predicting that Junior would be thrilled to see not just an actual ghost town, but one that is on top of an unquenchable underground coal fire and he happily asked endless questions about it, as a six-year-old is wont to do. Their three-year-old daughter, Sophie, was happy as usual, prattling incessantly as was her habit in the backseat while Junior talked about hopefully seeing some actual ghosts.

"Sorry to disappoint you, little man, but that's not exactly what that means," he told Junior. "It's not a town full of ghosts, it's a town where all the people are gone and only the houses remain."

"Aww, maaaaaaan!" Junior exclaimed, with an exaggerated pouty lower lip, as six-year-olds are also wont to do. "That suuuucks! Ghosts are wicked awesome!"

Ava laughed, but Adam rolled his eyes and pursed his lips slightly.

He loved both his children, but if he were ever to be painfully honest (which, Dear Friend, I have to tell you, Adam was typically not in so far as this is concerned) he'd have to admit he resented his son. He and Ava had been together since his first job at the *Sacramento Bee*, and for most of their marriage, it had been just the two of them, which suited Adam. They'd always had more than enough money, the resources and time and freedom to travel, and didn't have to share each other with anyone else. This is what really bothered Adam the most, that after Junior was born, he was no longer Ava's focus. When Ava, after so many years of talking about having kids, finally announced she was going off her birth control pills because, being over 40 by then, it was now or never.

Adam went along with her wishes even though he still wasn't sure he even wanted any children. He accepted Ava's desire for children, and understood why, and yet he still found himself with lingering resentment directed towards his son.

"OK," said Ava, her long, brown hair seeming to be wreathed by a halo in the bright, low-hanging November sun. "Tell me again where this is near, babe."

"It's right on the river...not too far from Deerfield, I guess."

"Deerfield? Hmm."

Adam glanced over to her as he drove, stopped for a minute by her loveliness before he spoke. They'd gone from very young adults in the early 90s to older adults, together now for nearly 30 years, but Adam felt the years had only enhanced his wife's beauty. The few gray streaks in her hair only seemed to contrast beautifully by her dark tones, and the small crow's feet etched in the caramel-toned skin at her hazel eyes made her smile even more infectious, he felt. Adam still loved his wife, after all these years.

But, for some time after Junior came along, this had not entirely been the case. The resentment Adam had first felt then had slowly grown, cancer-like, until they both had to admit there was something horribly wrong in their marriage. Earlier the previous year they had willingly gone to a marriage counselor because they both believed their busy lives and demanding careers were pulling them apart, and they desperately didn't want to lose what they had. In addition to Adam's work at the news network, Ava worked as a professor of social work at Boston College and as a researcher there at the Research Program on Children and Adversity. Add two small children into the mix, with their demands and schedules and nightly whining, and it had become all too easy for them to drift apart.

Spending more quality time as a family, and most especially quality time as a married couple, was one of the things the marriage counselor strongly suggested. Day trips to area fun spots was one of the things they both seized upon as a reasonable way to spend more time together, and have a nice time doing so.

"'Hmm?'," he said. "What's 'hmm' about Deerfield?"

"That's where the academy is, remember? They've been trying to recruit me to begin that development program there for years now. They're really persistent."

"Oh, that's right. Yeah, makes sense the Deerfield Academy would be in Deerfield. How 'bout that?"

"Makes perfect sense to me," Ava said with a smile.

As they turned from I-90 onto I-91 to begin going

northward, the view along the Connecticut River was just as lovely, in a somber November kind of way, as the countryside beyond Boston had been earlier. However, the further north they went to more low-hanging clouds blotted out the sun, until the bright golden beams became fully hidden behind a curtain of steel gray.

"You know," Adam said, after noting it looked like snow might be coming in, "we've been talking since forever about getting out of Chestnut Hill..."

"Yeah, that we have been," Ava agreed.

"I mean, I love the college town vibe and all that, don't get me wrong, but our house is so small, and everything is so damn expensive there." Adam swept his arm around, taking in the landscape. "If we were to finally move, maybe coming out this way would make sense."

Adam took the exit off I-91 for Deerfield, then worked their way around until they reached River Road. As a low-hanging fog wrapped misty arms around the car, Ava looked out the window and nibbled her soft lower lip gently. This was, Adam knew, a sign that meant she was thinking about something difficult. "It's beautiful, yeah, but...I don't know, babe..."

"What don't you know?"

But before Ava could answer, Adam saw the old, dilapidated sign welcoming them to what was once the bustling town of Cromwell's Ferry.

"Oh, wait – we're here," he said. "I guess we'll talk more about this later."

Adam slowed and turned off River Road down a random street to the right, and immediately had an intrigued yet eerie feeling as they crept along the husk of this former town. The paved streets, long since abandoned and no longer maintained, were pockmarked with deep cracks and potholes. Almost all the houses were gone, but often stone steps leading to now-vacant lots stood there still in mute testimony to the lives that were once lived here, and the community that once thrived in this place. Like a mansion that is abandoned and left to rot, the row after row of empty lots bounded by dilapidated, crumbling streets created a deep sense of melancholy, mingled with dread. The low-lying mist, ever-present and inexplicable, made the sense of sorrow hang even more heavily in the air, and made the wildly growing trees take on strangely threatening, twisted shapes in the gloom.

"Whoooooah," Junior said excitedly from the back seat. "Wicked!"

Ava looked back at him, and said, "I don't know. Makes me feel...sad."

Adam looked around, thrilled. He'd always loved a good mystery, and this relic seemed like one giant mystery just waiting to be unraveled. He drove around aimlessly for a bit until he saw what was once the parking lot for some small business and pulled into it. Nearby were some small, still-standing houses, though by the looks of their decrepit state Adam had no idea what was still holding them up. He supposed some old houses just had a will of their own.

"Come on," he whispered, to make the fun of exploring this impossibly quiet, spooky place more of an adventure for the kids, taking note that there were still personal effects from the various houses strewn about. "Let's go have a look around."

As soon as the family got out of the car, Adam noticed several things all at once, the most obvious of which was the cloying odor that hung thick in the air, almost like another layer of mist enshrouding this place. The rotten egg stink of sulfur was powerful, just as Teresa warned him it would be.

"Ewwwwwwwww, gross," Junior said loudly, pulling his long corn-rowed hair to cover his nose. "What's that smell?"

"Poop?" Sophie helpfully offered.

"No, that's sulfur," Ava said, clutching her coat around her more tightly. "It comes from the coal fire."

"It stinks worse than poop!" Junior said.

"Poopie-poopie-poopie!" Sophie suggested again, running around as if riding a horse.

Adam stood there, turning in slow circles to take in the whole thing. He didn't know why, but this place touched some part of him, perhaps some untapped explorer part of him that wanted nothing more than to dive into the unknown and discover whatever he could. He felt like this place was rife with undiscovered mysteries.

As he turned around slowly taking everything in, he noted the obvious sulfur odor, but also noted there were other, less powerful odors there, too. One odor that gently lingered in the air he thought was something reminiscent of his childhood, a smell oddly like burnt metal. He would often visit his father's parents in their small house during summer vacations, where his grandfather still worked in the same factory he had been since his return from World War II. Adam was never quite sure what his grandfather did there – all he really knew was that, whatever it was, his grandfather died from mesothelioma because of it – but he'd always have that smell on him when he came back from work. When asked by the curious kid he was, his grandfather would simply tell Adam it was the stink of burnt metal.

But under that, lingering even more gently than the burnt metal, was another, almost coppery odor. Given the mix of metals that were likely entwined the with coal this didn't surprise Adam at all, but he couldn't help thinking it smelled ever so slightly of blood.

"It's so warm here," Ava said, coming up to him now. Despite that, she clutched her coat still more tightly around her. "I can't believe how warm it is. It's got to be a good ten degrees warmer here, maybe more. This place is insane."

"I know, it's crazy, isn't it?" Adam agreed. "You can feel the heat right through your shoes, can't you?"

"Yeah," Ava said. "It's warm and…I don't know. Not humid, but it feels so…what? Close? Stuffy? It's like the air can't move."

Adam nodded in agreement and glanced at Ava as he did so and saw that, despite the warmth and still air, she clutched her jacket tightly to her, as if chilly.

"Are you OK?" he asked. "Why are you holding your coat like that?"

"Yeah, I'm fine. This place is just…weird. I don't know. I just feel odd here."

"Huh," he said, distracted by looking around. "OK."

Adam looked down now to get a closer look at the ground. He saw that the cracks he'd noted earlier, aside from being the normal breakdown of unmaintained asphalt, seemed to be peeling back or breaking apart as a result of the infernal heat. As he looked, he saw thin, wispy tendrils of whitish smoke limned with threads of pale green leak steadily upward from the cracks. He watched as the smoke drifted lazily up, swaying slightly in the still air, seeming almost to dance to some unheard music and to then be sucked back into the ground suddenly, only to begin again a moment later. It gave the ground, and the very earth itself, the look of a great sleeping beast, slowly breezing as it dreamed. Adam watched, mesmerized, and entertained by this strangely dancing smoke.

He looked up from examining the cracked and seething road to suddenly see looming, amorphous gray shapes hidden in the mist. He realized these were grand old houses, mansions from the indistinct look of it, that had somehow not been torn down yet.

"C'mon," he said to his family. "Let's go look around awhile."

"Dad," Junior said, taking Adam's soft hand in his own, the boy's previous unfettered excitement replaced now with a tone of apprehension in his voice. "What happened here?"

"Oh, my, little man" he said. "That is such a messed-up story..."

Adam gave him the thumbnail sketch version of the tragic death of Cromwell's Ferry. He explained how back in 1966 the town had been falling on hard times, going from a big industrial town to a mere shadow of its former self with just one factory left, a chemical company. Though details are sketchy, the chemical factory was apparently being run at beyond capacity production with just a skeleton crew to watch over things, when there was a massive explosion. No one really knows to this day what happened (well, no one other than me, Dear Friend, but that's literally another story) but the explosion was so large it demolished a huge portion of the town, and then much of what survived burned down in the subsequent fire. To make matters much worse, there were exposed veins of coal all through this region, and the fire burned so hot and for so long that it ignited the coal, which greedily dug deeper and deeper into the earth, connecting one burning vein to another. By the time anyone realized there was a fully involved underground coal fire burning beneath Cromwell's Ferry there was nothing they could do to stop it.

By the early 1980s Congress had allocated millions in relocation funding, and by the end of the decade, the governor had forced the last stubborn residents out by right of eminent domain. By then, only a handful of obstinate old-timers remained, but by the early 1990s, Cromwell's Ferry was nothing but a mist-enshrouded ghost town by the Connecticut River.

"Adam," Ava said after walking past several empty blocks and one overgrown cemetery with thin strands of foul-smelling smoke rising from the graves. "I don't like this place. Not at all. And the kids aren't feeling well either. I want to go."

He looked back at her and nodded in agreement, though he also kept walking. "OK, we can go in a bit. I just want to check out these houses, alright?"

The family walked westward as they strolled past one empty, overgrown lot after another. The closeness, that strange humidity Ava had noted earlier, seemed to be getting worse, the air becoming somehow even more stagnant than before. Yet on they walked, the houses apparently much more distant than Adam realized due to the mist; it must have been a strange illusion caused by the fog, but it seemed somehow that the longer they walked towards the houses the farther they seemed to be.

They were caught off guard suddenly by the growl-like sound of flames flaring up on their left, and saw, on a small hillock in an empty lot, the earth cracked open with flames suddenly pouring out. This enflamed crack was right in between two long since dead trees, their twisted and blackened limbs seemingly stretched upwards towards heaven, as if begging for this interminable torment to finally end.

The lot was surrounded by an old wooden snow fence for safety with postings to stay far away, but Adam thought someone would have to be a fool or insane to go anywhere near that. The unquenchable heat felt like standing in front of an oven, even though they were twenty yards or so from the rift. Despite the safety fence, Adam noted there was a broken baby doll near the rift, her plastic face melted just enough that she seemed to be screaming in pain. He assumed it had been left behind when the family who used to lived on this lot fled their burning town.

"Look at that!" Junior said, again excited by their adventure. "So wicked!"

Wicked? Adam thought. *How appropriate.*

Although he had no religious beliefs at all, if there were ever an actual gateway to hell, Adam would bet it'd look like this angrily glowing, oddly growling slashed cut in the earth. He saw bright orange and yellow and pure white embers blazing deep within the ground, flames of brilliant orange, blue, purple, and even green shooting out all around them, dancing wildly. That weirdly mixed stench of sulfur, burnt metal, and copper was stronger here than anywhere else.

As Adam told Junior the story of the town's death, he'd noted the increasing amount of graffiti on roads with wildly deteriorating conditions. When they first entered town there was something here and there spray painted on the ground, things that were painfully immature and clearly the work of bored teenagers – goofy smiling faces, peace signs, kids' names, and the ever-popular squirting dick icons. But as they walked on, the cracks in the roads deepened, looking more like savage wounds suffered in some ferocious fight, smoke now billowing out in a regular stream.

The painted graffiti also became far more regular, these roads – these smashed, ruined, utterly twisted roads – now covered in a complete jumble of graffiti, much of which seemed far more sinister than before. Adam noted the playful tone of the earlier work was gone, with not a squirting dick to be seen anywhere, instead being replaced with many strange symbols. He at first was willing to dismiss even these as just teenage nonsense, until he saw a perfectly drawn circle painted on the ground in bright red, with two bands of symbols surrounding it, and what appeared to be the burned bones of small animals scattered all around. He saw this as they passed by an intersection and was relieved to note no one else did.

Above all the other inane, incoherent symbols that seemed to be everywhere, Adam observed several places of very clear though irregular, almost insane writing. The first they passed stated *He is here* several times, followed by a few *He is watching*, each time next to two evil-looking eyes. And then, simply and finally, *Andromelech*.

Surrounding this strange word at the four cardinal points was an equally strange symbol, one that Adam suddenly realized had been spray painted all over the roads, and even the houses back near where they parked. The first time he saw it, Adam dismissed it as nothing but a scribble, but after recognizing it was connected to that word he understood it had been in many other places leading towards here. Though appearing as nothing but a few jagged lines that twisted sharply back and forth over itself several times that meant nothing to him, it obviously meant something.

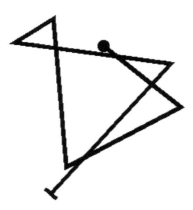

"What is all this?" Ava wondered in whispered tones.

"I don't know. It's neat but...weird."

Adam realized suddenly that they'd walked clear out of Cromwell's Ferry, the neat gridwork of town streets replaced by what was once a two-lane road leading into town. That one-time road was now nothing but a smashed and wrecked strip of twisted asphalt with bizarre things spray painted on it. Adam was shocked to realize the houses he thought they'd been walking towards the whole time was nothing but a large, wooded hill looming high above this entire area. In the mist, it's hulking frame and undulating spurs must have looked vaguely like houses.

He looked up towards the hill's mist-enshrouded summit just as one small spear of sunlight broke through the churning clouds.

"Adam," Ava said again, a tone of irritation and fear in her voice. "We need to go. Now. This place is scaring the kids. Look at them."

He was turning his head away from the hilltop to answer her, when he saw a sudden flash, bright and clear, from the peak of the hill cut through the mist and the leafless trees. He whipped his head around, surprised to find something flashing from atop the hill. When he did, he again saw the flashing, two quick flashes followed by a pause, then another two quick flashes. Then, the sun swallowed up again by the mist and clouds, the flashing stopped.

"What is that?" he said exclaimed suddenly. "What the hell is *that?!*"

"What is what?" Ava said, but even as she said this, Adam was already running up the hill towards where he saw the flashes.

"Adam! *Adam!* Where the hell are you going?! *ADAM... come back!!*" she yelled after him, but uselessly. Adam ran up the hill now, compelled by something within him that made no real sense, seemingly drawn forward by some force to find out where that flashing was coming from. Even as Ava's shouts for him to come back were swallowed up by the fog and his quickly growing distance, Adam focused only on moving forward, moving up the hill. The woods on the hill were not thick, so maneuvering through the gnarled and twisted trees was easy.

Adam, not knowing why, only knowing he had to, kept pushing further and further up the hill.

The hill itself wasn't terribly steep, but as he steadily worked his way up, he could tell it was massive and high. Adam kept pushing upward, rising above the low-lying mist around the town. Although the skies were still gray and cloudy, breaking through the mist made the day seem brighter and less gloomy. This emboldened Adam to work his way up the hill faster and faster, drawn on as if being dragged by some unseen thread, all but running up the slope.

Then, breaking through the last twisted saplings and breathing hard, Adam stepped out onto the flat, treeless hilltop, and saw it. He stood there for a moment, dumbfounded, wondering if this wasn't some bizarre hallucination or a heart attack brought on by the sudden exertion. Feeling dizzy, Adam closed his eyes, breathing deeply. He opened them, and still he saw it, feeling as if it were beckoning him onward, almost as if it'd been waiting for him for there the whole time.

What Adam saw on top of that massive hill, my Dear Friend, was an enormous, three-story brick colonial mansion. A grand portico ran almost the entire length of the central part of the house, four thick, huge pillars supporting a gabled roof. Steps surrounded the entire portico, seemingly hewn of solid blocks of stone. Many windows, with what could have been the original muntins for all he knew, pierced the brick walls. The windows of the first story were oversized, whereas the windows on the second story were normally proportioned, and the third story windows a bit undersized. On either side of the central, rectangular hub of the house were two smaller rectangular wings. Four large chimneys reached upwards from the roof, through what appeared to still be slate shingles.

Though lovely, the old house was certainly run down. The paint was faded and chipped, the brick stained almost black with years of grime, with ivy growing along portions of it, and the dead amber grass of the lawn long and beaten down. Despite all this, Adam thought this was the loveliest house he had ever seen in his life.

"Holy shit..." he said breathlessly, slowly approaching the mansion with a sense of reverence and awe. "Holy shit."

He walked slowly and cautiously, as if afraid he'd spook the mansion and it'd scurry off to hide once again in the woods. As he did, he heard a gentle squeaking sound and looked to see that of all the many windows in this old mansion only one was broken, and a small, singular shard of glass turned slowly in the dull sun. It was this one shard, he realized, that he saw reflecting the sunlight, causing the flashing that brought him there.

"Holy shit," he said once again. "What a coincidence." The shard, perhaps agreeing with his assessment, fell to the ground.

Still walking as if stalking the building, Adam now walked up the portico steps. Double doors, apparently once painted yellow and now a wrecked shade of flaking pale cream, stood as if welcoming him to the home. Though clearly uninhabited, he still couldn't just let himself inside the house to look around, though he did peek in through the windows. He saw a home interior that in many ways matched the exterior. Though dirty and clearly uncared for for years, with some of the old plaster having fallen to the hardwood floors, it seemed in remarkably good condition and was more beautiful than he could have imagined.

As he walked down the portico steps to attempt to look

into the side windows, he heard voices approaching, then rustling and steps approaching from the woods behind him.

"Adam!" Ava yelled loudly as soon as she made it to the clearing, carrying Sophie and all but dragging Junior. She was flushed, panting heavily, almost in tears, and clearly angry. "What the...what the...what the *fuck*, Adam?! Why did you run off like that? Why'd you leave me alone with the kids in that creepy place?!"

Sophie began to cry suddenly, tears streaming down her chubby ruddy cheeks, having apparently had a bit too much excitement for one day. Junior simply stopped in mid-step and, staring at the house, started sucking his thumb.

"Ava, I am so, so sorry," Adam said, kissing her on the forehead and taking Sophie from his wife so she could relax a bit. He bounced and soothed his suddenly very cranky little girl. "I seriously don't know what came over me. I just saw flashing up here and got caught up in the mystery of it and had to – I mean, I just *had* to – find out what it was. But I'm so sorry I ditched you like that."

"Well," she said, less red now and catching her breath, but still irritated. "What was it? What was this great freaking mystery?"

Adam turned, sweeping his free arm as if to present the mansion to her. "Take a look at this."

Ava had seen the house as she approached Adam but was so focused on her anger she paid it no attention. Now she looked at it closely. "Wow...that's amazing. You wouldn't expect to find a mansion like that near a burned-out ghost town, would you?"

"Yeah, apparently what I saw flashing was this one little piece of broken glass from the one window that's broken. Isn't that crazy?"

"What's crazy is that this house is still standing, actually."

Adam looked at her sharply. "What? What do you mean?"

"Look at it...aww, come here, Sophie," she said, taking her still-crying daughter in her arms now to soothe. "It was beautiful once, but long ago. This house is almost in as bad shape as that town down there."

"Huh...well, I don't know about that," Adam said. "I took a closer look at it, and it's beat up, yeah, but it still seems really solid. The foundation looks good for a colonial mansion – well, assuming it's actually colonial and not a reproduction."

"Well, hopefully, someone can fix it up. I mean, the view *is* gorgeous."

Adam had been so focused on the house that he hadn't noticed anything else, but now that he turned to look around, he realized what an amazing view the top of the hill afforded him. The mists around Cromwell's Ferry, though eerie and strange down in the town, from here seemed like nothing more than the gentle vapors rising from a pond on a cool autumn morning; it was just a beautiful addition to a gorgeous landscape. From the hilltop Adam could see the gentle curves of the Connecticut River slowly making its way past the town, he could easily see Sugarloaf Mountain and the Sunderland Bridge, and much of the countryside beyond all that. It was indeed altogether lovely.

"Wow...I hadn't noticed that. It is beautiful."

"Sure is. There's a for-sale sign over there, so hopefully, someone can save it from ruin."

"There's a for-sale sign?!" Adam asked, amazed at his weak powers of observation. He looked where Ava pointed and realized he'd missed the sign since it was hidden in the tall grass. Walking over to it, he saw the sign was old and weather-beaten, but it had a web address next to the realtor number listed, so it was at least somewhat modern.

He used his phone to take a quick picture of the phone number. He didn't tell Ava he did, nor, Dear Friend, could he tell why he didn't.

"Why is there a for sale sign?" Adam asked, suddenly realizing the oddity of it. "I thought all the houses were already bought up by the government."

"I don't know," said Ava. She looked back from where they had come. "The only thing I can figure is that this house is beyond the limits of the town, or maybe because we're way up on this hill the fires don't prove a threat to it."

"Hmmm..." he said. "Yeah, you're probably right."

"But," Ava said, "this place feels as humid and stuffy as it did down there in the town. This whole place just has a creepy vibe to it." She bounced Sophie, who had gone from mere crying now to screaming, while Junior had done nothing this whole time but suck his thumb and stare blankly at the house.

"I don't know, I kind of like it," Adam said, while thinking *This is literally the most beautiful thing I've ever seen.*

"To each their own, babe, but either way, it's time to go. Sophie obviously needs a nap and Junior is so tired he's sucking his thumb, practically catatonic. He hasn't done that in years. Can we please go now?"

"Umm..." Adam started, looking around, just aching to stay, alone if need be, to explore the house and lands. He felt like a dog who finally has a nice tasty bone on which gnaw only to have that bone taken away by a cruel owner. But rather than petulantly insisting on staying to explore, he simply said, "Yeah, sure. Of course. The kids clearly need some rest."

Working together, they managed the kids and made their way down the hill easily. Almost as soon as they did, Sophie stopped crying and Junior returned to his normal boisterous, inquisitive self. No, Adam had to admit to his son, he didn't know what kind of tree that was. Yes, he agreed that walking in dried leaves did indeed sound like eating potato chips. No, he really didn't think roasting marshmallows in these fires was a good idea.

They walked quickly through the remains of Cromwell's Ferry to their car and left this strange, wonderful, terrible place. Almost as soon as they pulled out of the town, both kids were fast asleep in their car seats.

As they drove southwards along I-91 the sun again came out again, a typical day of November weather in Massachusetts. Adam and Ava chatted comfortably on the way home, discussing the day they just had and the evening they had planned. The silences in between were calm and comfortable.

It was into one of these silences, as his mind continued to whirl endlessly about the house, the view from the hilltop, everything that could potentially be for them in that home, that Adam abruptly said, "I could see us living there."

Ava, snatched from her own reverie, blinked at Adam for a moment, then, with a chuckle, said, "In that house?"

"Yes," Adam said. He didn't chuckle at all. "Absolutely in that house."

"It's falling apart, babe."

"No, it isn't," he said sternly, not understanding why she was being so obtuse about this. "I'm no contractor but I looked it over pretty well, and it looks solid to me. Besides... we have some money. You know that."

"Yeah, OK, but..."

"But what?" Adam asked, growing strangely impatient with his wife.

"It's two hours from Boston, which is where both of us work."

"Yes, and it's so close to Deerfield it's in the school district. It's close enough to the academy that you could almost walk there if you wanted to. I can work from home most days, maybe go to the studio once a week."

"Well great, but...I still work for the college, not the academy."

"Ava, you know how much they want you. You could call them right now and say, 'How much will you pay me?' and they'll give you a figure that's as much as if not more than you make at BC."

"Yes, OK, I'm sure that's all true, but I don't think this a good idea. I think buying that house and moving our lives out here on a whim would be just unwise. Our lives are in Boston."

"I don't understand now," Adam said, getting irritated. "It's not a whim. We've talked about moving out this way. This would just be a totally unexpected way to do it, in a house we didn't even know existed, but everything, in the end, would be the same. So, I'm confused."

Ava thought for a moment and said, "But what about the cost? A house like that has got to be wicked expensive, and I don't see how we can swing that."

"Like I said, you know full well we're not hurting for money. In addition to our salaries, we have a whole lot of stock, and the stocks are all up right now. Plus, I'm still getting royalties from my book. We can totally do this."

Ava looked out the window, shrugging her shoulders as she again said, "Yeah, but...I don't know..."

"I just don't get what you don't know about," Adam said. "We'd be moving away from Chestnut Hill, which we've agreed we wanted to do. Check. We'd be moving to a gorgeous house in the country, which is one of the things we said we wanted. Check. We'd be moving to a place where you can get a job you said you were interested in. Check-check-check. I'm still a little confused here, Ava."

Ava looked out the window at the countryside as they now worked their way back east on I-90, chewing her lower lip again. What she couldn't find the words to express (and what, Dear Friend, she felt silly even thinking) was that she didn't want to live there because it felt creepy to her. The whole time she was in Cromwell's Ferry she felt like the air was so close and still that she could barely breathe, but it was far more than the oppression of a humid day. It had a strange, unpleasant feeling of...a *presence* was the only word she could find to express it, but then she felt stupid for thinking like that.

The oppressive feeling continued on the hilltop but added to it was an even stranger sense of being watched. Her eyes had kept darting to the many windows in the house, expecting to see someone leering at them. But the more she thought about these feeling the more foolish she felt, and she certainly couldn't express these feelings to Adam. They shared a lack of faith in anything that couldn't be proven by science, but he tended to be far less tolerant of those who did. She really didn't want to be mocked by her husband for feeling like there was something weird on that hill by telling him her concerns.

So, she didn't.

"I guess there isn't really a good reason," she said at last, "assuming everything works out money-wise. I guess it's just a whole lot all at once."

"OK," Adam said, smiling. "That I can totally get. It has been a heck of a day."

Ava nodded solemnly. "Yeah, it sure has been. So, how about this: Let's allow this to settle and for the emotions to calm down, and then we can think about this some more. Then, *later*, we can talk about it a bit more rationally. Sound good?"

"Yes," Adam said. "Sounds very good. Thanks for being open-minded about this. I appreciate it and I love you."

Bitch.

Adam recoiled as that word smashed into this mind, like

an ax slamming into his brain. He had no idea where it came from and was both shocked and ashamed at himself for thinking so disrespectfully of his wife, of becoming so irritated with her because she didn't want immediately to do what he wanted.

What the hell is wrong with you, Adam? You don't think about her like that!

They remained in a somewhat less comfortable silence all the way home, as Ava struggled with the strange feeling that there was something horribly wrong with that house, and as Adam dreamed of the wonderful things that could possibly happen for them in that same house.

[4]

THE NEXT DAY IN HIS OFFICE, ADAM WAS ON HIS COMPUTER checking website after website to learn more about the house as he sipped his latte. He should have been reviewing stories, checking assignments, approving scripts, and the many other things that constituted his job. Instead, he was obsessively feeding a gnawing need to learn more about this house. He had managed to get through his morning meeting with Teresa, but since then he had been looking up things online about the house on the hill. It was now well past lunchtime, a meal he'd missed in his tenacious pursuit of information.

He sat now at his desk, muttering quietly to himself as he took notes. "Alright...OK...what are you?" he asked his empty office.

He was surprised when he first began this search to find that not only was the house an actual colonial-era relic, it was one with some historical significance. There were numerous history websites that had descriptions of the house– which he came to learn was named Blackstone Manor – and its long history, mostly due to its importance in the early westward expansion of the state and its role in King Phillip's War. Adam was quite surprised to find that it was also listed on several sites that deal with historical crimes and murder houses.

"Well, alright then...a house with a backstory. That's cool."

It was originally built in 1680 by a man named Uzziah Blackstone, who was the first settler in that area. Although his was a classic colonial story – one in which he left Boston due to abject failure and crushing debt, went into the wilderness, founded a trading post that grew into a town, and then due to a combination of hard work, willpower, and ruthlessness transformed himself into a rich merchant – Adam was far more interested in the history of the manor house itself.

The original house eventually burned down, killing Uzziah and his entire family except for his eldest son, Cromwell. He rebuilt it and expanded it, living there for the rest of his long life; having no children who survived to adulthood, it was sold outside the Blackstone family. It passed from family to family throughout its long history, but though it passed through many hands over the years, there seemed always to be a history of tragedy associated with the house on Blackstone Hill. One of the sites Adam found hyperbolically referred to *The Curse of Blackstone Manor* to explain the things that kept happening there.

Adam chuckled to himself. "A 'curse,' eh? Yeah, I don't think so."

Curse or no, he did have to admit there was an above-average amount of death in that house, even by the standard in the eras he was looking at. None of Cromwell Blackstone's children lived past age ten, and almost all the subsequent families that lived in the house had death visit them swiftly, often, and violently.

"1763, mother kills children, then self...father kills himself," Adam muttered, taking notes on a large yellow legal pad, as was his habit. "1770, British officer hangs his wife, kills servants in their bedroom, jumps to his own death...1804, mother punishes children by making them stand outside naked in blizzard, they freeze to death, she kills herself...1810, adult son kills his father, kills mother, rapes sister, then kills everyone else..."

Adam put his pen down and sat back in his chair, arms crossed, rubbing his chin. "Huh. OK. This is...this is odd."

He scrolled through the long list of murderous entries he was reading, now skimming it rather than documenting every instance of violence. "1861...iron baron maybe abuses his servants, maybe he kills a few, maybe not, no one knows... 1875, father rapes teenage daughter and kills with an ax to the head...1891, father slaughters entire family, kills self in woods on hillside...1965, son gets killed in hunting accident, father comes back to shoot wife and remaining children, then drowns self in pool...1971, mother drowns all the kids in the pool..."

Adam stopped scrolling. He'd seen enough. The place certainly had an unfortunate history, but whereas that might terrify or dissuade the average person, for Adam, it just made the house even more intriguing. It was a house with a dark mystery behind it, and mysteries were something Adam felt needed to be revealed.

Don't mention this to Ava, though, he thought. *You know how sensitive she is about kids and their welfare. She wouldn't like that at all.* That, and *It apparently has a pool. Awesome!*

He returned to some of the sites that had pictures of it from about the mid-1800s, in which it largely looked as it does currently, aside from changes to the grounds. Adam then went to the realtor website from the for-sale sign and was thrilled to see pictures of the interior of the house. He felt vindicated because the photographs proved the damage was not terrible, especially for a house of this age, but at the same time the pictures revealed far more damage than he was able to see through the windows.

"No biggie, no biggie..." he almost whispered now. "We'll get it taken care of, no doubt about it."

Having done research on the house, having learned the history of it, seen pictures of it through the years, seen photos of the past and current interiors, Adam wanted to get inside of it terribly. He knew he was obsessing over this, but that was a trait of his he'd long come to accept and, as a reporter, even to cherish. Once he got his mind on something, he just could not let it go until he was satisfied. So, having done all the prep work, he now took what he considered the next logical step and called the realtor.

After some initial confusion regarding what house it was he was referring to, Adam was finally directed to a very excited realtor named Lilly. She said it had been some years that the house was on the market, and there hadn't been a great deal of interest in the home over those years.

He was initially most curious about the boundaries of the property and how that related to Cromwell's Ferry, so he asked her for clarification.

"Oh, yes, that's all very fortunate," she chirped happily. "You see, the federal injunction and property buyback covers only the town itself, and since the hill lies outside of town, well then, the government has nothing to say about that."

"Oh, OK," he said. "That is lucky. So, there's nothing getting in the way of it selling?"

"No, not at all!" Lilly said, perhaps a bit too excitedly. "Plus, to put your nerves at ease, the hill itself was studied in the 1970s once the fire came to light and all that, and it was found to be pretty much a cone of solid limestone. So, even if there is a vein burning directly under the hill it won't ever shift or burn because of the rock. It's totally solid, you see."

Lilly said she was thrilled that someone was finally expressing a desire to see the long-forgotten gem of a house, but while she would love to meet Adam the very next day as he suggested, there was no way she could get free to show it until the following week. Though he was disappointed, they made arrangements to meet there in a few days' time.

He was continuing to scroll through some of the murder house web sites to learn more when there were two quick knocks at the door, and then Teresa let herself into his office.

"Hey, boss, you have a minute?" she asked.

"Yeah, sure. What's up?"

Teresa closed the door behind her, and then handed him her phone. On the screen was a story from *The Washington Times* with a headline reading, "House Republicans call on ABC to explain why it spiked Jeffrey Epstein story."

"Have you seen this?" she asked him.

"Umm, no...I've been tied up this morning."

"Looks like Congress is going to begin snooping around, seeing who knew what and when they knew it, and if they were reporting what they knew."

"Yeah, I guess," Adam said, distracted with thoughts of the house and its history.

"And you...never had anything to do with any stories about him while you were at *A New Day*? ABC was the first to drop the ball on this?"

Adam suddenly wondered what office gossip had been going around since he'd gotten the email from his general manager the previous week, the irritation of that morning coming back a little. He leaned back in his chair. "I had some, actually. A reporter came to us about him, said she had the whole scoop, but the editorial board and management decided not to run with it."

Teresa sat down on the tweed couch next to his desk, then leaned on it towards Adam. "Listen, you know I have friends and contacts all over the place, in TV, print, on web sites, all over. I have friends on the right, left, middle, whatever."

"Yes, I know this," Adam said, getting a little annoyed. "You're very popular."

She ignored his snark, and continued by saying, "Well, one of my friends at this conservative news blog said they've spoken to a reporter who claims she went to your former employers in 2014 with the complete story about Epstein..."

"Yeah, which is what I just said."

Teresa put up one finger to stop him and went on. "Only thing is she's saying that *you* were the one who decided to quash it, and that you made her sign a nondisclosure contract before you'd buy her piece."

"Teresa," Adam said, appreciating her concern yet still trying to control his growing irritation. "I'm grateful you're giving me this heads-up, but this is nothing different than what I've already told the upper floors. I signed the contract with her because the editorial board..."

Teresa stopped him with her interruption. "This web site has the entire *New Day* editorial board on record saying they never heard of this reporter, nor of her report, that they would've run with the story had they known, and the whole thing...is your fault."

After a moment, Adam became aware of how stupid he must've looked, sitting there, with his bright blue bug-eyes open even wider than normal, his mouth half-open, the color draining from his face.

"Those fuckers," he hissed. Though Adam figured he had committed himself to this lie, and so he had to go all-in at this point, he was truly angered he'd never been contacted by this conservative news site. "They didn't try to contact me to comment on this."

"Look, boss," Teresa said. "I believe you. You know I do. But I just wanted to let you know that my friend told me they're going to publish this story tomorrow, that the editorial board is throwing you under the bus, and that the reporter is laying all this at your feet."

Adam sat in his chair, arms crossed, anger growing.

Teresa added, "I believe you, but this is going to look bad for you, Adam. The timing couldn't get any worse. Congress apparently wants to rip ABC a new one for passing on the story, but that was a more recent editorial decision. You're going to be accused of having had it *for five years*. I've been told the story is going to say lots of kids might've been saved if you had acted on the story."

Fuck them. Fuck them all, he thought.

Adam sat there seething with anger and growing hatred. He looked at Teresa. "Thank you for letting me know this. I do appreciate it."

"You're welcome, boss." She stood up to leave. "I'm going to leave you be now. If you need me, let me know, OK?"

"Yep."

After Teresa left, Adam wanted to smash things in his office to let off the angry energy he'd built up inside him, but since he could hardly do that, he instead sat there thinking about what this meant, growing angrier as he did so.

Adam thought about how he should proceed to manage this situation, to keep his job and maintain his professional reputation. He'd already committed himself to the half-truth he'd told before, so he'd have to stick to his guns about that. There'd be an internal investigation, of that he had no doubt, because that was protocol when something like this happened. For the internal thing, he'd just have to cleave to his story and make it seem like the editorial board at *A New*

Day was making a scapegoat of him, but if called before Congress what he really needed to do was find the conservative blog reporter and bury an ax in his head, and probably stab out his general manager's eyeballs, too.

Wait, what?! What the fuck?!! Where'd that come from?

Adam was surprised how quickly his thoughts turned from crisis management and reputation preservation to violent murder. He supposed it was due to the many hours he'd spent reading about the violence at the house, but even as he thought about this, perfectly formed images of wrapping his hands around someone's neck and slowly squeezing the life out of them, of burying a sharp knife deep inside their chest and watching the life leave their eyes, and chopping someone's face into pulp with an ax flashed through his mind.

He stood abruptly, looking around his office nervously, as if he expected to see someone there who knew what horrible things he was thinking. Adam was shaken by this sudden turn inside his own head. He'd never been a violent person and had certainly never thought of murdering people, so those bizarre flashing images confused him terribly; he thought the best thing to do would be to leave early for the day to calm down, rest, and plan for what was next. He recalled that he hadn't eaten any lunch, so believing that had something to do with all this, he stopped and got himself to a much-needed meal at the Chestnut Hill Restaurant.

Afterward he felt much calmer about the strange turn of thinking. He didn't have a similar thought for the rest of the day, and that evening, as he lay in bed thinking, he just accepted that it was an unusual turn into the darkness of his own mind under a moment of extreme stress and a little bit of hunger. *No biggie. People think strange things when they're under stress all the time. Ava has always said so.* This line of thinking calmed and soothed him as the evening went on, which he was able to then enjoy with his family.

And later, with the unabashed honesty that can only ever happen in those moments just before falling asleep, Adam admitted to himself he'd enjoyed the thrill of power that came from those violent thoughts and images.

[5]

THE FOLLOWING WEEK PASSED SLOWLY AND ANXIOUSLY FOR Adam. He'd emailed his general manager to let her know what would supposedly be published the next day on that news blog, and indeed it was. The story detailed the claims originally made by the reporter in the story she'd sold to Adam while he was at *A New Day*, as well as her additional allegation that he'd bought it just to quash it, as evidenced by the fact that she had to sign a now five-year-old non-disclosure agreement. Just as Teresa had warned, the *New Day* editorial board emphatically stated they'd never heard about the story and that the decision to quash it was all Adam's.

As expected, the general manager told Adam that once the story broke there'd have to be an internal investigation into the allegations. He was thankful that he would not be suspended during the investigation, though he was not permitted to engage in his usual producer duties. These were transferred to Teresa in the meantime, and his daily expectations were extremely indistinct. Nonetheless, Adam continued to report to work every day, believing he might be of some value if needed.

46

He found the turmoil arising from the internal investigation far easier to manage than the excited anticipation he had to deal with until he could view the house, though the boredom at work didn't help at all. Adam had found himself obsessing over the house ever since he'd come back from accidentally stumbling onto it, thinking about possessing it, about making it his. He'd been having trouble sleeping since then because of his mind racing with all the possibilities in the dark, quiet stillness of the night. He'd begun to feel as if the house were his constant companion.

Since he had so little to do at work, Adam had been doing much of the same there as well. He'd go to his office, open his email, several news sites, and stock pages he typically monitored each day, and then fall into a trance-like reverie, staring at the computer screen. He'd picture an imagined future for him and his family living in Blackstone Manor.

He saw some future Christmas, a fresh layer of snow blanketing their hill and all the surrounding countryside in postcard picture perfection, a huge Christmas tree in the living room brightly decorated, surrounded by piles of presents. He could see the joyous looks on his kids' faces as they ran downstairs to tear into their presents, Ava following behind with an almost serene look of blissful contentment on her face. They were all nattily dressed in bright reds and greens. He looked at Ava in deep love, and she looked back, smiling, with love and appreciation in her eyes for him finding their family this beautiful home. Later, he could see them all happily playing in the blood-stained and gore-smeared snow.

He jolted himself back to reality with a sudden cry that he quickly covered with a few forced coughs. He looked around wildly as had done on the first day he'd had those intrusive violent thoughts, less disturbed than he had been then, but still confused. This had been happening more and more frequently, where his at first wholesome thoughts about future family bliss turn twisted and perverted. Yet despite the thoughts becoming somehow tainted he found he couldn't stop going back to his fantasies about the house, each day passing the same way, the thoughts themselves only becoming more and more terrible.

As that long week passed, his daydreams turned so that there were no longer moments of an idyllic family acting out some perfect scene but were instead twisted from the beginning. Adam still imagined the lovely family moments of holidays and birthdays and bright summer days spent in the pool, but now as he looked at the faces of his family it was as if the smiles were too big, the too-wide-open eyes pleading for an end to their misery and pain. As he watched, he saw his family with cockroaches, oversized centipede-like creatures, and other horrific things he couldn't identify crawling all over them, scrambling into their mouths, up their nostrils, pushing into their eye sockets, burrowing into their flesh to slide just under their skin, all while the family had no reaction other than to smile all the more widely, eyes begging all the more earnestly for a swift end. Each time he'd snap himself out of these visions, only to go back again and again.

Adam was concerned his lack of sleep was beginning to affect his mental health. He was eager to finally see the house because he was very certain all would be well if he could just get inside the house and look around.

On the day of the appointment with Lilly, Adam showed up to work as usual, opened his email and the news sites, soy latte in hand like normal, and drifted off like he had been. He once again watched as those crawling beasts blanketed his family members, who didn't react at all other than to smile insanely at him. But today his daydream took on a new and far darker turn when he saw himself having sex with Ava. His musings had been growing more sexual, then more perverted, as the days went on, but today the perversion became violent.

He watched in his mind as he threw Ava face down to the hardwood floor, his hand tightly squeezing her throat tightly, closing it off. He took her violently from behind and could feel her dryness, and because in his fantasy Adam was forcing himself upon her, he found the pain he caused her delightful. Far more delightful was feeling her blood begin to act as lubrication due to his brutally cruel thrusting as his hand crushed her throat even more, until she was thrashing to get away from him, gasping for breath, eyes bulging, tongue sticking out.

This time he sat bolt upright, staring wild-eyed at his many unopened emails, heart pounding, breathing hard. He sat there, simply staring at the screen, covered in a thin layer of slick sweat, the image of his dying wife's blackening face slowly fading from his mind. As his breathing slowed, Adam became aware of the fact his cock was steely hard and throbbing greedily in his pants.

It was time to leave if he wanted to get to the house with plenty of time, which he did. So, without bothering to tell anyone in the office, he left for the day, careful to hide the giant bulge in his pants. He retraced the path they'd taken the week before, this time avoiding entirely the remains of Cromwell's Ferry on another road to access the long stone driveway that curled its way around Blackstone Hill like a corkscrew. As he made the final turn to the long straight portion of the driveway leading to the house, he had a sudden feeling of being home after a long, unwanted separation.

He pulled up to the house, noting with some annoyance that Lilly wasn't there yet, even though he was 45 minutes early for the appointment. Adam got out and decided to sit on the portico steps. Though the stone was cold, the day steel gray and chilly with the threat of a bitter rain later, sitting there on the steps felt very comfortable for Adam.

Home. I'm home.

As he sat there with his eyes closed, listening to the slight breeze whistle through the tall treetops, Adam could smell a very gentle earthy odor coming from the house. Earthy and moist, in the way that only an old house could smell. It was an odor that took him away to his youth growing up in rural southern California, a place where he never felt welcome nor at home, but one that always had that same earthy smell to it.

He was the son of a writer and English professor at a community college, and an artist and progressive political organizer. His beliefs did not match those of his school peers at all, who were mostly the children of the area ranch hands and farmers. They did chores; he learned about political movements. Their hands were callused; his were soft and always holding a pen to write. They were physical and active; he was intellectual and introspective. The called him pencil neck; he called them hicks. They hated him, and he utterly loathed them in return.

Escaping to Berkeley was the best thing that had happened for Adam up to that point, and even though he loved his years there, he was always a temporary interloper and so never truly felt at home there, either. Neither had he felt truly at home in Sacramento, nor in Washington, nor even now in Chestnut Hill. Adam had always, to a certain degree, felt like a square peg pounded into a round hole, ever the outsider.

He didn't know what it was about this old house atop a lonely hill, but here he felt at home. Here was the place to raise his kids and grow old with Ava. Here was the place to make a life. Breathing the odor in deeply, he opened his eyes as he heard a car approaching. It was Lilly, arriving ten minutes early for the appointment.

"Oh, my," she said, getting out of the car and happily shaking his hand. "I didn't expect you to be here already. I'm so glad you're here."

"Yeah, I've been pretty eager to see the house and wanted to get here early."

"Alright then. So, first of all, I have to ask you: Are you aware of this history of the house?"

Adam said he was, having looked it up online and researched the manor's entire long and admittedly bloody history. When asked if that dissuaded him at all, Adam assured Lilly it did not.

"Oh, wonderful," Lilly said, finally unlocking the door. That wet, earthy odor Adam had smelled on the porch was much stronger inside, but not unpleasantly so. It was warm and the air inside still, but the scent just seemed to be welcoming Adam home. "That's just wonderful! You see, this is the sort of thing that might concern some people about buying a house with such a history. There are even some people who say it's haunted."

Adam raised an eyebrow at that foolishness. "Oh, really?" he said, looking at the large foyer. Though everything had been modernized over the years in terms of electric, heating, and plumbing, the original colonial style of the house had been preserved. He was pleased to see that. The foyer occupied the central portion of the main hub, with a black and white tiled floor leading up to a large staircase leading to the second floor. At the top of the staircase, a balcony wrapped around and went to either side of the house, taking someone to either wing, allowing a view of the foyer from above. Looking up, he saw a modern, electric version of the original iron chandelier pending there...the one, as he recalled, from which a few former residents had hanged themselves. "Some people think it's haunted, eh?"

"Yes, some do. Now, I've been here several times before,

sometimes alone. I can tell you I've never once heard or seen anything, though I will also tell you I have had a sense of being watched a few times. But I guess that can be normal in any large, old house, right?"

"Mmhmmm," Adam agreed, distracted by the details of the house and not really paying attention to her prattling. The walls of the foyer were coffered wood, and Adam now touched the smooth panels as he slowly walked deeper into the foyer, thinking of all the history these walls had seen. As he looked down, he realized that what he at first thought were modern tiles were actually black and white marble, with small flecks of gold and strands of smoky gray entwined in the black marble, whereas the white had what looked like iridescent cream colored threads limned throughout it. Though covered in some broken plaster dust and grime, Adam thought the floor was simply gorgeous. Working his way to the rear of the foyer, Adam now saw there were double French doors in the back of the house leading to a colonnade, with the pool beyond and a large, potentially lovely yard beyond that.

Adam slowly and carefully took the tour of the entire massive house. He wanted to check out every little detail and to not merely see the house but indeed to truly *feel* it. After the several hours he spent there, it felt like home more than ever.

The house was indeed beautiful but having now seen it in person he realized there was thousands of dollars' worth of repairs that had to be done. He had been correct last week when he'd told Ava the foundation was secure and the house in good shape, given its age. However, that didn't mean there weren't many things that needed repaired, replaced, or updated, and none of that would be cheap or fast.

The last owner of the house was an artist who died in 1997, Lilly had explained. Since then, his estate had repaired the damages he'd done to it during a wild psychotic break, but after doing so it only used the house to store the paintings and writings he'd produced while living here with no regular upkeep to the property. So, there was over 20 years of neglect that had to be addressed before the house could truly be livable again.

However, the upside of that was the estate wanted to get rid of the house, and so was willing to part with it for pennies on the dollar; it wanted a price that was a fraction of what Adam had expected. If they did make the decision to buy this house, paying for the repairs had suddenly become far more affordable.

On his way home, Adam called Ava to tell her he'd be a little late getting home from work. He'd told her he needed to go talk to a potential confidential source, something producers don't normally do, but he implied this source had deeply sensitive information he'd only share with Adam. Ava always respected the confidentiality of his work sometimes required and never asked prying questions, just as he had done when she was a clinical social worker in private practice. He used her trust now to his advantage.

In the same way he didn't know why he'd kept hidden the fact he'd gotten the realtor number from Ava when they were at the house last week, he didn't now know why he was still not being honest with her. Whatever the reason, he just didn't feel like this was the right time to tell her.

I will, at the right time, Adam assured himself. *At the time right time. Not yet, though.*

Whenever that time might be, Adam did not truly know. All he knew for sure was that he slept soundly and deeply that night, with dreams about nothing but a bright, beautiful future.

[6]

TWO WEEKS INTO THE SPRING SEMESTER AT BOSTON College, Ava sat in her McGuinn Hall office on a cold January afternoon as slanted beams of the early afternoon sun cast long shadows on the wall. She sat at her desk feeling overwhelmed as she juggled grading papers, reviewing withdraw requests, reading emails from students, considering research proposals, refining her own research, and checking on her students' field placements. Things would calm down, or at least she hoped they would, after the first few weeks. But at this very moment, she wanted to pull out her wavy brown hair.

It was in this temporary maelstrom of higher educational angst that she heard Adam's voice at her office door. "Knock-knock, Doctor Rotenberg-Long. Can you use your social worker superpowers to save this lost soul?" he said, closing her office door behind him and sitting in the chair across from her desk. He smiled bemusedly at her disheveled state. "Or, from the looks of it, do you need saving?"

"Hey, you! You are a sight for sore eyes, let me tell you that. What are you doing here?"

"Well, you know the kids had their doctor's appointments today."

"Yeah, how are they?"

"Junior's fine," Adam said. "I still think he has ADHD or something, but the doctor said he's really just an average six-year-old boy. He wants to give it a few more years before prescribing him anything."

"Well, good," Ava said. They'd had this discussion many times in the past, my Dear Friend. "I keep telling you there's nothing at all wrong with him, babe. Little boys are just naturally a little...well, crazy. He's just your run-of-the-mill rambunctious boy."

"Maybe, but he's always all over the place. It can be annoying."

"So maybe *you* need medication," Ava said, with a chuckle.

"Ha!" Adam laughed. "Maybe I do. Gimme them drugs, doc. Gimme them drugs!"

Ava laughed along with her husband. "Sorry, babe, not that kind of doctor. And how about Sophie?"

Adam beamed, happily. "She's perfect. Just a happy, healthy, perfect little three-year-old girl."

"Of course. How couldn't she be coming from such awesome parents?" Ava joked.

"I know, right? Well, I dropped Junior off at school and Sophie back to daycare, and while I was in the area *anyway*..." This was something of a sarcastic joke on Adam's part. Not long before Christmas he was informed by company management that the internal investigation was largely inconclusive, and it was a matter of two believable sides of the same story. So, because of that ambiguity they didn't feel it was appropriate to fire Adam. However, that same ambiguity made keeping him in his current position untenable for the company, due to the "optics" of it, so he was being removed from his producer position and kept on as a political consultant at the same pay grade. It was a fair deal, yet Adam was still angered and slighted by it because he felt he'd done nothing wrong. He now worked from home and so was *always* in the area, answering emails from Teresa and guiding stories rather than truly crafting them, which was his passion. "...I got you some lunch," he said, holding up a paper bag from the Chestnut Hill Restaurant.

"Oh, is that a hot pastrami sub in there?" Ava said, eagerly.

"Mmhmmm...and fries." Adam said, nodding. "Do I know my wife or what?"

"You do indeed."

Ava greedily unwrapped the sandwich, taking in the glorious odor of it, suddenly aware of how hungry she was. She took her first bite of the sandwich and was about to comment how perfect it was, when Adam blurted out, "I bought it. I bought the house."

Ava looked at him, chewing slowly as she tried to figure out what he meant. She stared into his enthusiastically wide-open eyes, the smile on his face not matching her excitement because she had no idea what he was talking about.

"You bought...the house? The house...the house on the hill? The one in Cromwell's Ferry?!"

"*Near* Cromwell's Ferry, but yeah. That one." His smile grew until Ava thought his face might break, while her mind still reeled with not fully understanding what was going on. "Isn't that great?!"

Ava was literally speechless. All she could do for a time was stare at him from across the desk, dumbly, until she again found her voice. "Adam, I don't understand."

"What don't you understand? The house...I bought it."

"What I don't understand," Ava said, growing angry at his sarcasm, "is that we said we were going to talk about it. Before any decisions were made, we were going to talk about it. On the way home that day, that's what we agreed to. We haven't talked about it at all since then, so I assumed you thought otherwise of it. Now, out of nowhere, you just tell me you bought it?!"

His smile faded, but his blue eyes locked onto hers unflinchingly. "Yep, I sure did. It's ours now."

"Without even *talking* to me about it? Without even – wait, how did we buy a house when I haven't signed anything?!"

"Yeah, well...I wanted to expedite the process as much as possible, so I just bought it. It's in my name."

She looked at him slack jawed, angered but also painfully hurt, then looked away.

"I mean, we can always amend the deed later, that's no biggie," he added. "But for now, yeah, it's only in my name."

Ava felt almost dizzy because of the train wreck of emotions she was feeling right now. She was confused about what had possessed Adam to make this rash decision – rash, and yet methodical at the same time, because he'd clearly been working at this since November – but she was also angered that he'd cut her out of this very important process. Entwined through all of that was a hurt the likes of which she'd never felt in her marriage before that day. Adam had always been very conscientious of her thoughts and her wisdom, and they'd always approached every decision together as a team. Now he was suddenly dictating to her that this major purchase had been made, and made in his name alone, no less. While there was certainly an entire swirl of negative emotions going on about this, the one she felt the most acutely was heartache.

That, and a creeping, gnawing fear, one in the darkest corners of her mind, but one she had to admit was there. Adam had never acted like this before, had never been as wan and distant as he had been for the past few months, and this change in personality frightened her terribly.

She looked at him now with tears welling up in her hazel eyes. "I just don't understand how you could do this huge thing and not even tell me your plans, let alone discuss it with me like I'm your wife," Ava said, now crying freely.

"Ava..." he said, reaching out to her from across the desk. She pulled away from him.

"No!" she yelled loudly, more loudly than she intended as the emotion took hold of her. Ava's tears flowed freely as she tried to talk around her sobbing. "I can't believe you did this to me...you didn't even consider me or my emotions...about how I might feel or what my thoughts are...how could you?!"

"Ava," he said again, but again she rebuffed his efforts at soothing.

"And how the fuck is this even supposed to work? You work from home, which is just *great* for you, but I still work here. Or have you forgotten that?!"

He simply stared at her mutely.

"Or maybe you just didn't care about me and what's convenient for me, as long as it suits *your* needs." Ava didn't think she'd ever been this viscerally hurt and angry at Adam before, perhaps never in her life. A new issue flashed, like an epiphany, into her mind. "A how are we even to pay for this? We already have a mortgage here, how can we swing another?"

"Well," Adam answered calmly, recognizing how hurt she was by his action. "First of all, the house was owned by an estate that had had it for years and they wanted to get rid of it, so I got it for, no lie, about one-quarter its assessed value."

"Of course, they did! It's a piece of shit," she said, intentionally trying to push Adam's buttons. She wasn't proud of herself, my Dear Friend, nor was this her normal personality, but she was furious.

Adam stood up now as if to leave, though he paused with his hand on the doorknob. "I sold some stock to buy it outright. There is no mortgage."

Before Ava could even comment on this, Adam went on, turning to her now. "Look, I know I've acted...differently. I know I cut you out of this decision. I know I've hurt you by doing this, and I am truly, deeply, so, so sorry."

The way he said that "so, so sorry" made Ava think of that day in November when they'd gone to Cromwell's Ferry and he'd run away up the hill. Once she'd caught up to him, angered at being abandoned and left with their two small children in a hell-scaped ghost town, he'd apologized just like that. *I am so, so sorry* he'd said then. She was suddenly afraid that day had marked the beginning of a very different husband and an equally very different marriage for her. Ava wasn't certain yet if this was the beginning of a glorious new chapter for them, or the beginning of the end.

Adam approached her slowly now, almost looking like he was afraid she'd punch him if he got too close, and then knelt next to her so he could gently take her hand in his as he spoke.

"I know I've done all this to you, and I will beg your forgiveness for the rest of my life if I have to. But I just need you to understand..." Adam paused, tears welling up in his eyes now. "This house, stumbling on it out of nowhere like that, it felt like...like a chance to have something real, a second chance, someplace I could really call home. You know how I've felt my whole life, never feeling...right, never feeling comfortable. This house, despite its *many* flaws, this can be our home, our dream home."

He put his hand on her cheek as he spoke. "I've felt like this could be a new beginning for us," Ava lifted an eyebrow as he said that, as it matched her own thoughts so closely. "Things at work have gotten so...messy. I know my reputation has taken a hit. It's ruined, actually. In a lot of ways, I'm afraid, *really* afraid, my career in journalism is over. Things here are so beyond hectic for you. We can start over there. I've been wanting to do a book on the impeachment, and I know in your heart you *want* to work at the academy."

Ava, despite her anger, had to admit that she did, she truly did. She knew being a program director at a prestigious boarding school would have many challenges, but she also knew the pace and demands would be far different than what she had now.

Adam pulled her head gently towards his, until they were forehead to forehead, as he spoke now in nothing more than a whisper. "We can spend more time together as a family. Things can be calmer and less hectic at home. We can actually have the time to enjoy our kids for a change rather than rushing around all night because everything is so crazy. Ava, please forgive me, I know I hurt you, but please know I felt like I had to this, I had to do it for me, I had to do it for us." As he finished, one single tear slowly traced its way down his smooth cheek.

He looked at her now, his blues eyes blazing intensely. "Please...I need you with me for this. We can do this."

Ava wanted to be angry at Adam for what he had done, she wanted to push him away and tell him to go fuck himself, but she hugged him instead.

"You know I'm with you, always," she said through her own tears. "You've hurt me by doing this more than I can ever express, but I can also forgive you for it...in time. Look, we still have *much* to talk about, and we do need to talk about it before any other decisions are made, but I can understand where you were coming from. I get it."

Adam wiped the tear away from his cheek, again taking his wife's face gently in his hand. "Thanks, baby. Thank you so much."

He stood and walked back to the door. "I'm going to go now. You clearly have a lot of work to do, and I'm sure there are loads and loads of uber important emails waiting for me to get on. Yep. Super-dooper sure that's the case."

Ava chuckled at his obvious lie. "What's done is done," she said, not even sure if she was referring to the house or his work situation as she said it. "We'll make it work."

Adam smiled at her and said, "We always do."

Ava remained in her office, turned away from her desk staring out the window at the snow-clad campus below her. The massive amount of work she needed to do had been as utterly forgotten about as the now cold pastrami sandwich. Things were about to change in her life – things had already started to change, she reflected – and she wasn't certain she liked the direction in which they were going.

With her mind still reeling several hours later from their conversation, the implications of Adam's duplicity, and the details of how they would make this work, Ava made her way down to where a commemoration ceremony for some martyrs was being held she wanted to attend. Though she usually skipped such events at the Catholic university where she worked, the martyrs being remembered in this case were also social workers, and so Ava felt she should be there due to professional solidarity if for no other reason.

As she passed through the hall's gothic rotunda, she saw her friend, Father Patrick Donegal, hands clasped behind his narrow frame, as he seemed to be pondering the statue there of Saint Michael defeating Lucifer. Although they had always disagreed on practically every important issue, from faith to politics, their relationship was one of deep respect and true affection. His years of dedicated service working with the poorest people from all over the world, especially children, made it difficult for Ava to hold him in anything but the highest esteem.

With his lean features, closely cropped salt-and-pepper beard, and his long hair tied into a tight grayish manbun, Ava always thought he looked more like one of her fellow social work professors should look than a Jesuit priest. She repressed a laugh as she approached him, these amusingly silly thoughts a pleasant diversion from her unhappy recent mindset. "Hi, Father Donegal," she said.

Her greeting seemed to snap him out of some deep thought. "Oh, hello, Ava," he said in return. He adjusted his round wire rim glasses before looking back up at the statue. "The struggle of good against evil. It really is quite an amazing thing, isn't it?"

Her eyes followed his up to the massive statue of an almost beatific looking Saint Michael, winged and clad in ancient armor, his sword poised ready to strike a prone Lucifer, on whose back he triumphantly trod. On Lucifer's face was a look that somehow combined horror, rage, and inexpressible frustration all at once. It was a look, Dear Friend, very much like the one he had on that day so long ago.

"Yes, it is an amazing statue," Ava said. "It's a remarkable piece of art."

Donegal glanced at Ava with a slight smile. "Yes, the statue itself is gorgeous. Even remarkable, as you say. But that's not what I meant."

She looked at the priest. "What did you mean?"

He thought for a moment before going on, still looking up at the statue. "I was reflecting earlier today on the nature of evil in the world, and so was struck once again by this statue. How huge and powerful and overwhelming evil is, and what can we do to stand against it? What can we do when it's bigger than us, yet what other choice do we have *but* to stand against it?"

Ava looked back up at the statue, then repeated his words

in almost a whisper. "What can we do?" she said, as, for just a moment, that gnawing fear and distant dread about Adam stirred in the darkness of her mind again. "Well, Patrick, I guess as a priest taking a stand against evil is definitely your field of expertise."

Donegal smiled at that. "I've served in parishes and schools all over the country, Ava," he said, looking at her now. "I've served all around the world. I've seen people living in truly wretched conditions, people who, despite that, still have deep faith and an abundance of hope in their hearts. And the one thing I've always taken away from those interactions – aside from the need for me to be a better and more devoted believer myself – is that their suffering is not by accident, and it's not mere chance. There are powers of evil in the world that have put them in these conditions, powers who benefit greatly from their suffering."

He paused, looking back to the statue. "Evil is a very real thing in the world, Ava. It is in the heart of mankind, it's in our very core. Evil is very real and very much something we *all* need to fight against."

She now looked at the statue again, but from a different mindset. As she thought on what Donegal said, she noted that Saint Michael, though victorious, was noticeably smaller than Lucifer. Was that an attempt to capture demonic proportions, she wondered, or was it a subtle message that, while we might feel weak and small, we do have the power to overcome any evil?

Are we, though? she asked herself. *Are we really able to defeat anything? Aren't there some things out there that are just bigger than we are? Is fighting and not winning enough?*

As her mind continued to wander around this issue of morality, of good and evil, of the struggle between the two, that deep gnawing turned to worries about that house and her husband. Ava felt like the house had an unnatural hold on

Adam, almost as if it had possessed his mind. Though it was mad and utterly bizarre, she couldn't help but feel that he had been different since that day in Cromwell's Ferry, almost as if the real Adam had been replaced and she'd been living with his double since then.

She refused to believe in alien abduction, and there is no way she would consider anything of a supernatural explanation, despite that creepy feeling of being watched while atop the hill. And yet, though she couldn't put her finger on it, *twisted* was the only word that seemed to adequately describe how Adam had been since that day. Her husband had become a twisted version of himself.

Maybe there was black mold in the house when he went to look at it, Ava thought, as her highly rational mind tried to find a logical explanation for the change in Adam's personality. *Maybe he breathed some in and it's been affecting his brain since then. I've heard about that. It can cause brain damage and change personalities. That would explain a lot.*

"Ava," Donegal said softly, bringing her back from her reverie. She didn't realize how long she'd been lost in her own thoughts, though it must have been some time as he was looking at her with true concern in his eyes. "Are you alright? You look...distraught. Is everything well?"

She glanced away quickly, tears suddenly welling up in her eyes again. In a rush of jumbled words and a venting of emotion, she explained that she and Adam had had a fight not long before she came down to the rotunda. She'd withheld some of the more important details, but Ava essentially emptied out the emotions that had been vexing her since Adam left.

"Oh...my," Ava said, after the flood of words and emotions tumbled out of her. She took a deep breath and held it a moment before exhaling and carrying on. "That does feel better. See? This is why therapy works so well."

"Therapy, yes...and confession," he added with an avuncular wink. "I am truly sorry this is happening to you two right now, Ava. Tonight, when I say my evening Rosary, I will dedicate it to you and Adam, that you might work things out and that your marriage would continue to be a blessing for you and your children."

"Thank you, Patrick," she said. "I do appreciate that." Ava smiled at Donegal and gently squeezed his arm in gratitude. Though she didn't share his beliefs she also knew his prayers were said in sincere faith and with deep concern for her wellbeing, so she wouldn't be anything but grateful for them.

Together they went into the auditorium for the commemoration service, but Ava's mind wandered the entire time. Perhaps it was because of the news that was suddenly dumped on her earlier, or perhaps because of the fight that ensued, or even just because she was overwhelmed at work. Whatever it was, regardless of how irrational it might be, she couldn't help but feeling small in the face of something infinitely larger and vastly more powerful than she.

[7]

WINTER SLOWLY TURNED TO SPRING, AS IT INEVITABLY always does, and in time the spring turned to summer. Adam hurriedly made his way along the highway to the house on a warm June day to check on the renovation progress, which he'd been doing with far greater frequency as the months went on. It'd been since January that Adam had contacted a Boston architect who specialized in historical renovations, who in turn hired a contractor with great experience working on old colonial houses like Blackstone Manor, and, though well within the average time to do such a project, he was growing impatient with the wait.

Adam wanted (no, my Dear Friend, he *needed*) everything to be absolutely perfect for the house, so his demands for perfection and an obsessed attention to detail had been growing with his impatience. He knew full well he was driving the work crew insane with his demands, and the foreman, Jimmy, was about at his wit's end with Adam. Yet, nonetheless, his once-monthly visits became twice monthly, then weekly, and now twice weekly.

As he raced along I-91 towards their soon-to-be home, he

66

thought about how things had been progressing over the past few months. Part of the slow approach was simply the realities of restoring a brick house that was well over 300 years old. It was not something that could be feasibly rushed, no matter how much Adam wanted it to be. Part of the delay was Adam himself, in that he insisted things be restored, in as much as was possible, to the original colonial appearance of the house. Gutting and modernizing rather than restoring would have been much faster, but Adam was amazed at how much of the mansion retained the original colonial elements. He just couldn't bring himself to be the one who ruined the house's historical appearance.

It truly was Adam making all these decisions. Ava had deliberately taken a hands-off approach to the house. She and Adam had worked things out since their fight in January, she'd eventually forgiven him, and even accepted that a move to the Deerfield area was inevitable because she'd accepted that job at the academy, but she'd also made it clear that she didn't want to get involved in the renovation planning. That was entirely Adam's responsibility.

Ava also made it clear that while she might accept the upcoming move, she still didn't like the house, nor did she feel nearly as comfortable there as did Adam. On the few times she'd been out to see the progress with Adam she had always noted how listless and still it felt inside the house, how the air was close just as it has been in Cromwell's Ferry. She admitted that it might improve once the house was all opened and a breeze could flow along the house, but for now she found it uncomfortably stuffy. Ava also shared with him she had an uneasy sense of being watched, but he dismissed her fears as just the weird feeling of being in a strange new setting.

Her tepid enthusiasm for this great adventure was

irksome to him, but he supposed he had to allow her that given he bought the house without even telling her his plans.

As he drove along and thought about that, it reminded Adam how his original plans were to be moved in by May, which Jimmy had initially said was at least technically feasible. However, one of his ongoing irritations with the renovation was that crew members kept quitting precipitously. He knew enough about construction to know individual workers came and went all the time, but there were several instances in which Jimmy told him work had to be shut down for days at a time because he'd had to hire a whole new crew, then shut down for a few more days because he's had to hire a whole other new crew a week later, because everyone would walk off mid-shift, or leave at the end of the day and simply never come back. Jimmy had told him he'd never experienced anything like this before, which had led to the unavoidable postponement.

Adam was also irritated that there were delays caused by many accidents, or at least what seemed a far above average number of accidents on one worksite. Thinking about that now, he recalled off the top of his head there was the worker who'd accidentally cut his hand off with a miter saw, the one who nearly drowned in the newly revitalized swimming pool, the one who fell off the ladder when the feet suddenly gave out and who then also pitched off the balcony to crash on the marble foyer beneath him, and the one who somehow managed to nail his own left hand to the wall.

The overall greatest delay, though, and the most irritating, was when a worker was killed. He was repointing the masonry on the chimneys when he apparently slipped on the slate shingles and plunged straight down three stories. To make matters worse, there was a backhoe loader on-site at the time, its scoop elevated high into the air. The man landed full on the elevated tines of the scoop, his frenzied shriek ending suddenly as the tines tore into his guts, literally ripping him in half. His legs lay crumpled on the ground before the loader, his torso in the scoop, as pink intestines and other organs dangled gaudily and disgustingly from the scoop tines. The bright yellow of the construction equipment was plashed in smears of vivid red blood.

Work shut down as the state and OSHA, as well as multiple insurers, annoyingly investigated the accident. Adam recalled the man was a migrant worker from Mexico, the kind his father intentionally chose to teach English to at that small community college in California. All in all, he wished the man had stayed the hell in Mexico, because his ghastly death had set back renovations by at least a month, perhaps more. Adam couldn't stand that much wasted time.

He pondered all these delays as he drove to the house, getting increasingly irritated but also excited to see the progress that had been done. He knew on some level he was being like a little kid eagerly awaiting Christmas morning, and, too impatient for his own good, kept focusing on how long Christmas was taking to finally get here. But, like the little kid, he didn't feel there was anything he could do about it. As he began to drive up the corkscrew portion of the driveway that curled around the hill, Adam drove faster and faster so he could get home.

He slowed just enough at the tight curve with the straightaway to not tip the car, yet nonetheless he did spin out a bit making the turn, sending white gravel showering everywhere. With the sudden appearance of a wildly careening car coming up the drive, every construction worker on site looked his way; he could practically feel the collective sigh when they realized who was coming. As he drove up the straightaway and around the new, oval-shaped portion of the driveway they'd added just before the house, Adam spotted

Jimmy and waved. Jimmy stamped out a cigarette and nodded unenthusiastically.

"Hey, Jimmy," Adam said, approaching the foreman as he dismissed the worker he was talking to. "How's progress going?"

"Adam," Jimmy said, arms spread out slightly, appealing to Adam's reason. "It's been three days. Not that much progress to be made in that time."

Adam looked at Jimmy darkly. "I'm getting impatient, Jimmy. Seriously impatient. I want to get myself and my family moved here as soon as we can. How much longer will this be?"

Jimmy sighed and looked around, rubbing his stubbled chin as he did. "As long as things go right – and so long as I don't lose any more crew – I'm thinking late July, early August at the latest."

"Late July?!" Adam exclaimed loudly, almost yelling. "You have to be kidding me, Jimmy. That's almost two months away!"

"I know that, Adam. But there is so much work to be done, and there is only so fast we can go on a project like this." Jimmy put his hand on Adam's shoulder reassuringly. "Nothing to do in a case like this but be patient."

"Nothing to do in a case like this but be patient," he says. What he means is "Shut up and go away." Fucker. Dumb, demanding worker bee fucker.

"But there are a few things that we were able to wrap up since last you were here that I can show you if you want."

"Yeah, alright," Adam said begrudgingly.

Jimmy showed Adam around outside first, pointing out that all the white crushed gravel for the driveway had been lain and that the house was finally repointed. That work was stopped altogether for several weeks following the death, so having it complete felt like closing an agonizing chapter is this long story. In addition to a few, minor aesthetic jobs completed, Adam was thrilled to see the fence around the pool was done and the new concrete around it fully cured, making the back yard of the house complete. That pleased him greatly as he thought about all the fun they would have playing out there as a family.

Once inside, Jimmy showed Adam the slow progress they were having removing every single old copper or lead pipe from the massive house and replacing them with modern plastic piping instead, ones far less likely to burst should the pipes freeze in a brutal Massachusetts winter. Not only did many of the pipes have yet to be replaced, but after that, the air would have to be bled out from the entire system, all the seals and gaskets checked, and then the many access holes in the walls would still need to be covered, patched, and the rooms painted. Adam was thankful for the new piping detail, and would certainly appreciate it come winter, but right now this snail's pace was driving him insane.

Perhaps seeing the foul look on Adam's face, Jimmy said, "But one really cool new thing today: We put that table together like you asked us to."

He looked at Jimmy confused for one moment, then said, "Oh, you mean the stone table?" Jimmy nodded proudly, smiling.

Several weeks ago, the crew had been working in the basement installing a drain and a new sump pump, gently contouring the brick-covered floor downwards to better direct flowing water to the drain. A significant amount of bricks had to be removed in order to angle the floor downwards properly, exposing the bare earth beneath it. As the crew dug into the dirt to deepen the sump pump pit and add additional drainage pipes, they were surprised to run into a block of solid stone. It turned out to be two separate pieces of what appeared to be granite, blackened and charred from the fire that had destroyed the original manor all those years ago.

Though chipped, cracked, and clearly damaged by fire and age, intricate shapes and writing of some kind could still be made out on the long, rectangular piece the crew first pulled out of the wet-smelling earth. They then pulled out the second piece, a gently tapered block that clearly fit into a slot carved out of the underside of the rectangular piece. Just as damaged as the first piece, this support block also had wildly eccentric carvings all over it.

When the work crew found the granite pieces, Jimmy had called Adam to ask what he wanted done with them. To Adam it sounded like they formed a table of some kind, so he thought it would be a cool addition to have it repaired and secured in one of the storage rooms in the basement. Jimmy now explained that they'd power washed off as much of the dirt and soot as they could, then epoxied the two pieces together and glazed the complete piece to protect it. Finally, they'd bolted it to the brick floor in the room Adam wanted.

"That thing isn't going anywhere, I can tell you that," Jimmy now said to Adam.

"Awesome. Let's take a look," Adam said, walking towards the door that led into the basement. He stopped and turned when he realized Jimmy wasn't coming down with him. "You coming?"

Jimmy looked at Adam without answering for a moment, then said. "No, sorry. I'm not going back down there."

Adam came back to where Jimmy stood. "Why? What's going on?"

Jimmy looked away, clearly searching for words. "I...I saw...something...down there the other day. Something... something weird. Not natural."

"Jimmy, what the fuck are you talking about?"

Jimmy now grabbed Adam by both shoulders, suddenly

showing more intensity and passion than he'd ever seen the foreman express before. "Listen, Adam. There's something very wrong with this house. I heard some of the guys talking about it, some of the things they've seen and heard. They said they'd seen ghosts and...other things and...and...well, just weird shit. I told them they were crazy or hungover or tripping on meth or whatever. But then, last week, down there, I saw...*something*."

Adam, shocked by this sudden outpouring of intensity and bizarre emotion, looked into Jimmy's wild, wide-open eyes, fearing for his mental health. "What'd you see, Jimmy?"

He let go of Adam and stepped back, again scratching his chin before going on. "I saw...a man."

"You saw...a man? A man in this house with a work crew full of men in it?"

"Yeah, look," Jimmy said, chuckling nervously, "I know how crazy it sounds, but this man wasn't one of my guys. He was young, wearing a real formal looking suit. He just stood there staring at me, like...like the way an animal looks at something it wants to eat." Jimmy looked away from Adam with a far-away look in his eye as he relived this event. "He just stood there staring at me, and all the while I feel this... horror is the only word for it. *Horror*. I felt a horror, a terror like nothing I've ever felt before, not even when I was in Iraq, not even in the middle of a firefight."

He paused, continuing to look away, now speaking in a harsh whisper. "Then he spoke to me, but it wasn't in words. He just showed me things, like...like...pictures flashing in my mind, the most horrible, violent things...I don't even want to think about it."

Adam thought for a moment about the terrible visions he'd also had in that long week between finding the house and being able to see it and wondered if Jimmy also wasn't sleeping. He was about to offer advice about sleep habits, when Jimmy said, "So I'm not going back down there. Not for a million bucks. No way in hell."

"Is all the work done down there?" Adam asked, again instantly focused on the renovation work.

"Yeah, it is. Listen, Adam: There is something very wrong with this house. I don't know what it is, but it's terrifying. I don't think the 'accidents' we've had here have been accidents at all, and I don't think Pablo's death was an accident, either. Not really. This is our work and I'll see the work done, but I'm telling you I'm never going back in that basement. And my advice to you is as soon as this renovation is done put the house on the market. You'll make a killing by flipping it, but don't *ever* move your family into this fucked up place."

Jimmy's unsolicited guidance rubbed Adam the wrong way, which hardened his heart against the advice. "Is the table in the rear room, where I wanted it?"

"Yes, it is. Right where you asked for it."

"Fine," Adam said, flipping on the lights as he descended the steps.

The colonial cellar was one of the things Adam found so amazing and attractive about this house, a truly unique aspect of it. Brick walls and floors, with the original rough-hewn timbers supporting the floors above exposed throughout the ceiling, the basement was as unique as it was utilitarian. Like any other colonial cellar, it was originally divided into several rooms used for food and other supply storage, so Adam thought there were innumerable uses to which he and Ava could put this space.

The basement occupied the same footprint as the original manor built by Uzziah, which is now the main central hub of the house. As he stepped down from the last stair, Adam had what was once the kitchen of the home on his left, a single wide-open, spacious area with a fireplace on the far wall. To his right was a long hall with the various storage rooms on either side of it. He'd asked that the table be placed in the farthest room at the end of the hall, which is where Jimmy said it was now bolted to the brick floor.

As he walked down the hall, the only thing he could feel was the chill of an old cellar, and all he could smell was damp earth. It felt like any other old basement he'd ever been in. He had no idea what kind of superstitious nonsense the work crew believed in, nor what kind of medication Jimmy obviously needed to be on, but there was clearly nothing down here but a colonial cellar.

Adam opened the creaking door to the rear room and looked at the granite table. Superstitious beliefs or not, he had to admit the work crew did an excellent job refurbishing the table. While certainly showing its age – though it was clearly there when the original house burned down, there was no telling if the pieces predated the manor – it looked fantastic. Although in his mind he'd been thinking about this piece as a table, now that he saw it, he thought it looked more like the altar at a Catholic church than anything else.

He stood at the door, arms akimbo, admiring the piece for a moment before striding into the room. He wanted to run his hands along the rough gray stone, to trace the carved curves and swirls in the stone with his fingertip – but as soon as he touched the cold stone his entire body tensed, as if he were being electrocuted. He stopped, frozen, his body tensing and contorting painfully as image after image of unbearable violence flashed through his mind.

Adam saw a torch-lit night many centuries ago on this hilltop, when tribes that long predated the Pocumtuc people, tribes that are now dead and long forgotten, lived nearby. He heard drums being hammered rhythmically, people chanting in time with the pounding drums. He saw a man holding a crooked tree branch with a jawless human skull affixed to the end of it that he was using as a staff, wearing long, black wolf furs as robes and buck antlers like a crown. As he chanted incantations, captured women from some other long-extinct tribes (he didn't know how he knew these details, my Dear Friend, but know them in that instant he did) were dragged from wooden cages and raped at the wolf mage's feet, then their throats slit. At the same time, captured men from the same tribes were dragged out of similar cages, forced to kneel with their heads against this very stone, and then killed by having them smashed with heavy clubs into a bloody pulp. Their brains and blood filled the etched curves, clogging the swirls with gore. He watched and saw as the bodies were dragged away to near the woods ringing the hill, to then be skinned and eaten by members of this victorious tribe.

He saw all this in an instant. Then, just as quickly, his mind flashed to another scene. He knew the year is 1763, and he also knew the owner of the home is a rich merchant named Richard Bates. He is returning after a long business trip to Boston, and as he opens the door to his home he is greeted by the sight of his wife, Catherine, dead for ten days by that time, hanging from the iron chandelier in the foyer. Her tongue sticks out of her mouth, blackened and bloated like the rest of her, as her bulging, dead white eyes stare at him unceasingly. The odor of rotting flesh hangs heavily in the stifling air of the house. Flies hover around her, land on her, in her, as maggots crawl all over her, burying themselves deep inside her skin. Again, Adam knows without knowing that Richard will soon find his children in their beds, murdered by his wife, and in his intense grief, slit his own wrists.

Another flash. Adam knows the year is 1822, and the house is being run as an orphanage by a woman named Rosa Kreuz. She takes great pleasure in having some of the older children physically abuse the younger ones, though she sometimes accords special torments to the children she particularly doesn't like by personally whipping and caning them in the vast cellar of the house. For the boys she especially despises, Rosa has a room set aside down there where she delights in using variously sized implements to rape their tender bodies.

Yet another. Adam knows its 1875 as he watches a man named Samuel King in his blood-stained suit slowly walking along the balcony, whispering and laughing to himself, dragging a bloody ax behind him. Adam knows this man had just murdered his wife with that ax and is going to rape and then murder Elizabeth, his teenage daughter. He knows all this, without knowing how he knows.

Again, another flash. It is now 1912, and a woman named Evelyn St. Germain has just gotten done stabbing her husband, Mortimer, several dozen times. She did this because she caught him in the attic quarters having sex with Carmella, one of the servants. Evelyn tells Carmella that she can choose to either be stabbed to death like Mortimer or to take her chances jumping out the window. The servant, a poor young girl just recently arrived from Sicily and not more than seventeen years old, shrieks for mercy and says she was being raped by Mortimer. Evelyn, however, doesn't believe Carmella nor does she care. Evelyn forces her to decide, slashing out with the knife to emphasize her seriousness. The girl, in a frenzied panic, decides to jump out the window and lands three stories below with a sickening crunch. Carmella is not dead, but broken so badly she can't move, and instead merely cries out in agony, her painful screams cutting through the black night. Adam watches as Evelyn calmly comes down from the attic to where Carmella lies, crumpled on the ground below, begging for mercy and help. Instead, she slowly begins to make long, shallow cuts into Carmella's smooth olive-toned skin, slicing off long cords of her flesh. After torturing her for so long the night sky started to turn bright with the approaching dawn, Evelyn finally stabbed the young girl to death in a fevered, frenzied attack. Evelyn happily surveys her bloody handiwork, then slits her throat, falling on top of Carmella.

A final flash and Adam knows it is now. He watches through his own eyes. He is in the chessboard-floored foyer, where he sees his children laying on the floor, covered in blood. In his bloody hands he holds an ax, and before him he sees Ava cowering in fear. A look of anguished pain and dread on her face, she slowly backs away from Adam with her hands out, trying to keep him away even as she begs to not be killed. He brings the ax back, and with all his might brings it down deep into her skull, cleaving her head into two pulpy halves.

At that moment Adam collapsed to the floor, exhausted. He lay there shaking in horror, his heart racing from the terror he felt watching those vivid images and from his now weakened muscles. He knew that all those flashes, even with the many intricate details, lasted less than five seconds, yet nonetheless he deflated when he hit the floor, totally drained, trying desperately to catch his breath. He had never seen such images of violence, not even the images he'd imagined previously. Adam rested on the floor, sweat now pouring off him despite the chilly air, catching breath and gathering his strength for about ten minutes before he felt strong enough to move again.

He stood up shakily, looking around, as if expecting to see a thin young man hungrily staring at him. He saw nothing but the brick walls of the room, and the granite slabs he'd had made into a table.

What the fuck was that? he asked himself, finding no answer in the echoes of his own mind. *What the fuck just happened to me? Am I going insane?!*

Adam refused to accept there was anything supernatural going on in his house – indeed, that there ever anything supernatural going on anywhere – and instead convinced himself this was some powerful psychological reaction to the story Jimmy had told him before viewing the granite table. He cleaved to the idea that this was essentially a delusion foisted upon him by the foreman. The more he thought about this perfectly obvious conclusion, the angrier he became, suspecting Jimmy had made up the entire story and done it purposefully to get him to stop checking on the progress so often.

Fucker. Worthless, worker bee piece of shit fucker! Just like those Neanderthals I had to grow up with. They thought it funny to tease me about my eyes, and now this fucker thinks it's funny to tell me stories to scare me. Damn worthless working-class piece of shit!

He adjusted his rumpled clothes, gathering himself, and pushed any explanation for this strange event other than a psychological one out of his mind entirely. Adam slowly climbed up the stairs, a deep muscle ache now taking over his entire body.

At the top of the steps Jimmy stood waiting. "Well?" he asked. "You were down there a long while. What do you think?"

"I think that table is absolutely perfect. I think you guys did a terrific job cleaning it up and securing it, and I think it looks great."

"Thank you. I appreciate that."

Adam then took one shaky yet aggressive step towards Jimmy, the anger for what he'd convinced himself was a deliberate attack overtaking him. Standing close enough to Jimmy he could smell the last cigarette the man had smoked, Adam said, "And I also think you'd better get this fucking job done as soon as you can, then get the fuck off my property. If you ever come back, I will fucking kill you. That's what I think."

[8]

THE BRUTALLY HOT MID-AUGUST SUN BEAT DOWN ON ADAM
mercilessly, the humid air making every movement feel like
slogging through a swamp as he hauled box after box from his
car into the foyer of their new home. The light tee-shirt he
wore was soaked with sweat and clung uncomfortably to his
hot skin, his hair a wet, sloppy mess. His muscles ached and
his heart pounded in his chest. The house still smelled like
moist earth as it did on that first day, but now it also had the
odor of new construction, sawdust, and oppressively
humid air.

Since the confrontation with Jimmy two months earlier
Adam had stopped coming to check on the progress of the
repairs, and in the last days of July he'd received a terse
message from the architect saying all repairs were done, and
he hoped they satisfied Adam's standards. He'd gone there
the next day to inspect everything and was pleased to note
that the superstitious bunch of apes they'd hired to get the
work done had managed to get every detail right. After a final
official inspection by the state, the house was free for them to
move into.

Every day for the past two weeks Adam had been packing up as much of the smaller things as he could on his own – Ava was unable to help in the moving process because she had to juggle transitioning out of her position at Boston College and into her new one at the Deerfield Academy – and so all the movers would have to get were the larger items. They'd decided to keep the first house as a rental unit, which meant everything needed to be cleared out as soon as possible.

He'd wake, get the kids to daycare, pack up everything he could, drive two hours to Deerfield, spend several hours unloading, then drive home another two hours to pick up the kids from daycare again. He was getting very tired with this process, in part, because he was feeling overwhelmed by how much stuff they'd squeezed into their small Chestnut Hill house, all of which had to be packed up and hauled to their new home, and but mostly because he was doing this entirely on his own.

Adam understood Ava was tied up with the juggling act of stepping out of one demanding position and into a new one, yet nonetheless, he felt abandoned by her. Moving is always a loathsome duty, more so during an oppressively hot summer, and Adam had assumed he'd have some help getting this endless line of boxes moved. But, no, that proved to be wrong. Ava had apologized profusely, but she said there was simply no way she could manage the transition *and* help him move.

He was on his own.

"Yeah, just like always," he grumbled to himself, hauling yet another box into Blackstone Manor to lay in the foyer. He'd load up his Subaru with as many boxes as he could possibly fit in there to reduce the number of trips he'd have to take, yet despite that, he felt like he was making no headway emptying the house at all. All it did accomplish was to make each load up and unload even more terrible. Adam was feeling alone, adrift in a sea of boxes, and he griped to himself about the unfairness of it as he just about melted in the summer sun.

"Why am I always doing shit alone?" he muttered to himself, lugging in a heavy box of books – *Why do we have so many books? Why do we read so fucking much? Hasn't anyone ever heard of a fucking library?!* – and putting it on the foyer floor just seconds before it slipped out of his hands because of the weight. Then, like an automaton, he'd turn around and grab yet another box. He stopped to take a sip of his iced latte only to spit it out again; all the ice had quickly melted in the ferocious heat and now he was merely drinking a heavily watered-down latte.

"Typical," he said. "Can't I *ever* get a little fucking help around here?"

He thought about how he'd done this whole thing on his own as he carried box after heavy box into the house. Even though it was completely by accident, *he* had found this house. *He* is the one who'd contacted the realtor, *he* is the one who'd viewed it, who made the decision to buy it, who'd sold the stock to make it a reality. This was entirely of *his* own doing, and now all the thanks he gets for making this gorgeous home theirs is to work like a slave in the unrelenting heat.

"FUCK!" he screamed aloud in frustration, to the empty hilltop.

As hot as it was outside, it was somehow even more so in the house, despite the fact all the downstairs windows were open in addition to the front and back doors. The architect had told him colonial houses like this were always built in such a way to catch as much breeze as they possibly could and to channel it wonderfully. In an era long before air conditioning, this was how colonial mansions were cooled. He'd assured Adam there'd be a delicious breeze running straight through the house, meaning the modern central air unit could likely be used sparingly.

"Well, guess we can add to the long list of things you're wrong about, motherfucker," he griped as he entered the house again, feeling a stifling heat and humidity that somehow made the outside conditions delightful. The air inside the house was so listless and still that it was almost like Adam could *feel* the pressure of the air itself pressing against him as if there were two or three rooms worth of hot air stuffed into that one single space. He put the heavy box down, looked at the wide-open front door, then the equally gaping back doors, and put out his hand to feel the breeze. There was none to feel. All that did happen, however, was a single fat drop of sweat fell from his arm to the floor with a wet *plip!*

"Fucking great," Adam said, his frustration now palpable.

He went outside to grab the last box, which turned out to be the heaviest. It was an overly large box full of books, so it was hefty, awkward, and he had to walk in an uncomfortably crouched way to squeeze the bottom closed. As he did, Adam thought about his many recent disappointments, including the Epstein story debacle, the *New Day* editorial board sacrificing him to save their own skins, the way the network had made him impotent in a job that was useless nothingness, Ava's refusal to help him, her utter lack of enthusiasm about the move, the way Jimmy had intentionally taunted him with a ridiculous ghost story, and about how the architect somehow fucked up the airflow. Adam was now murderously angry as much as he was physically tired and drenched with sweat.

Despite his best efforts, just before he put the box down the bottom burst open, spilling the books everywhere. He threw the box as he again shrieked "*FUUUUUUUUUUCK!!*" in extreme frustration. Adam plopped himself down on the cold marble floor, holding his sweaty head in his hands, eyes closed, feeling defeated and frustrated.

He sat there cross-legged, feeling the blood throbbing in his temples. He slowly took deep breaths and tried to calm himself as he listened to the bugs chirping outside and the complete silence in the house.

Adam snapped open his eyes and lifted his head suddenly when he realized that there wasn't *actually* complete silence in the house. Now that he was sitting there quietly, he heard something, but he couldn't quite make it out. Adam stood, turning his head slightly to one side to try to hear it better. The sound was there, but it was tantalizingly just under his ability to make it out clearly – when in an instant he realized he heard someone in his house whispering.

Despite the heat, an electric chill of fear ripped throughout his body with the realization that someone must have snuck into his house through the back door while he was distracted carrying in boxes. He feared that perhaps this was some insane homeless person wandering the woods around his hill, or maybe some spaced-out drug addict. Either way, Adam grabbed his largest golf club from the bag that was still in the foyer, and slowly crept his way towards the now clarifying whispers.

As he turned his head slowly from one side to the next to determine from where it was coming, Adam could tell the intruder was in the room off the foyer to his right. He slowly walked in that direction as stealthily as he could, golf club held high like a sword. The door to that room was ajar, and as he approached, he could hear the whispering now more clearly, though he couldn't make out what the intruder was saying.

Must be some crazy, he thought. *Babbling nonsense. I'll crush his skull if he makes a move towards me.*

He stood now at the door, listening, and with one quick motion pushed it open and stepped into an empty room.

Adam stood in the doorway, club in front of him now, eyes scanning the empty room. "What the fuck?" he asked out loud, but even as he did, he realized the whispering was coming from one of the wing rooms beyond where he now stood. He assumed the house had weird acoustics given its shape and size, and he had yet to learn these little nuances.

Adam now crept along the short passage connecting the wing to the central hub and came to the closed door of the room. As he stood there listening, with his hand on the doorknob, he was surprised to realize there were *two* voices whispering. Suddenly feeling more apprehension at the idea of having to take on two possibly crazed homeless people, Adam swallowed hard and girded himself for the fight he'd have on his hands. He whispered a countdown from three, then burst into the room with a blood-curdling scream, golf club raised high.

Only to find this room as equally empty as the first.

"What the...what...what the *fuck*?" he stammered, his confusion now growing.

Yet even as Adam stood there, eyes scanning the empty room for where someone could be hiding, he now heard a chorus of whispers coming from the foyer.

"No, no, no!" he yelled now, no longer creeping along but instead walking quickly towards the foyer. When he suddenly burst into it, it was empty, and he spun around and around trying to comprehend what was happening to him.

"This isn't happening...this isn't happening!" he said, his voice becoming more and more of a shriek. "This cannot be happening!!"

As he stopped spinning, he could now hear more voices whispering in the wing rooms to the left of where he'd originally started.

"WHO ARE YOU?!" Adam said in a full-throated yell as he ran towards the leftward wing. "WHO THE FUCK ARE YOU?!! *I'LL FUCKING KILL YOU!!*"

He ran all the way to the left-wing of the house, finding empty room after empty room. Yet despite that, the whispering continued unabated, more and more voices adding to the incomprehensible cacophony, a crashing together of words he couldn't possibly decipher.

Crazed now with a combination of fear, denial, and refusal to accept the obviously supernatural content of what was happening to him, Adam ran out of the wing rooms, tossing aside the useless golf club, racing through the foyer again and running upstairs, going from room to room trying to find the source of these voices, which only grew louder and more insistent as he did so.

He ran, sweat flying off his now blanched skin, his eyes wild with fear, trying desperately to find these voices. He ran through the entire attic checking each room, going to the front room window, the one out of which Carmella had leaped all those years earlier, to see if perhaps someone were outside pulling an elaborate prank on him using speakers. He saw no one, and still, the voices grew in number and intensity.

Adam raced downstairs to the foyer, crazed like a wild beast when it suddenly realizes it is finally trapped by hunters and soon about to die. The sweat still poured off him, now no longer due to oppressive heat but rather a pure animalistic panic, his eyes racing wildly, trying to make sense of the incomprehensible. He clapped his hands over his ears, unable to abide the sound of these eldritch whispers any longer.

Worse perhaps than the inexplicable whispering, was the utterly vicious malevolence he felt in that cacophony of voices. The murderous hatred and loathing he sensed surrounding him were like nothing he had ever experienced before and was something he suspected could never normally be felt in our everyday human existence. It penetrated him, making him suddenly nauseous, dizzy, and shaky.

He stood there impotently in the foyer, hands over his ears, feeling as if he were going mad, feeling as if his head were about to burst, on the verge of tears. Adam screamed his throat raw saying, "Stop! Stop, STOP, *STOP!! STOP, STOP, STOP-STOP-STOP!!!*"

Just as Adam felt like he would lose the last thin tendril of sanity to which he was still desperately clinging, all the voices abruptly stopped, plunging the house back into complete silence. He stood there, hands yet clasped to his ears, looking around like a tortured animal does when the torment finally stops, unwilling to quite believe it's over. He slowly let his hands down from his ears, his racing heart starting to slow, his breath approaching normal, the nauseous feeling melting away.

Holy fuck, he thought. *It's true, it's all true. Jimmy was right, Ava was right. This is no place for a family!*

As the primal panic melted out of him and Adam felt he could move again, he quickly ran to his car. He left both doors and all the windows wide open, but he didn't care one iota. The homeless, the crazies, the squirrels could have the house for all he cared at that moment. His only thought was getting out of there as quickly as possible.

He started the engine, having every intention of driving home and telling Ava what had happened, and that it was best they not move into this house after all. He stopped, however, his hand hovering just over the gear shift as he heard now one clear, distinct voice whispering to him.

One voice whispering to him, a voice he couldn't help but hear and obey.

Adam sat there, staring out the windshield without seeing, a glassy look to his eyes. His mind was filled with a great many other visions instead. As he stared, Adam smiled slightly, tittering to himself, finding the plans being laid out to him delicious in their simplicity and yet audacious in their scope.

His fear was replaced with a knowingness and a dark joy of the inevitable.

"Yes...yes, of course, I'll do it..." he now whispered back to the disembodied voice, again tittering, his mouth curling into a crooked smile. "Yes...I will do so. I *do* want that, yes. Mmhmmm...everything. Yes. Of course, I will do it...yes. Yes. For you...yes."

After some minutes of this, the voice ended, and Adam returned to himself as if nothing at all had happened. He calmly went back into the house, making sure to close and lock every window before neatly piling the books that had fallen. Adam felt no fear, no trepidation; it had all been explained to him, and he felt nothing but wonderfully at home. He understood now why the air always felt so close in the house, and simply accepted it as part of the uniqueness of his new home.

Adam locked both doors, then happily walked out to his car. He put it in drive and headed home, humming softly to himself. He felt proud about the work he'd done that day and looked forward to letting Ava know he was nearly done getting the boxes moved. Adam had also started working on the book he'd been planning and felt like the move to the hilltop would be the best place for him to focus on hammering it out before the elections. He looked so forward to moving his family into their gorgeous new home.

And now he *really* looked forward to all the family fun that would soon happen after that.

[9]

"GORGEOUS, SIMPLY GORGEOUS," AVA SAID AS SHE LOOKED out upon their new back yard and the view beyond.

Adam and Ava sat comfortably on some new wicker furniture on their colonnade. They both sat there, sipping wine, enjoying the gorgeous view from the hilltop on this refreshingly cool mid-September evening. The landscape of the entire Connecticut River valley around them was alive with bright fall colors of reds, yellows, and golds, mixed in with some stubborn summertime greens. Adam knew the peak colors for this part of the state would be in about another two weeks, and he looked so forward to seeing that from their hilltop.

Today marked their first official day in the house. Earlier in the day, Ava dropped off Sophie at her new pre-school program, Junior to his new first-grade class at Deerfield Elementary, and then went to her job at the academy. Meanwhile, Adam stayed back in Chestnut Hill to meet the movers, who'd managed to pack all their furniture and other large items in no time. Together they drove to the new house, where the movers unloaded as quickly as they'd packed up their truck.

Adam had spent the rest of the day putting away as many things as he could, focusing primarily on the kitchen, bathrooms, and bedrooms. When Ava returned home later in the day – it was still bright afternoon, they both were pleased to note, and not well into the evening as it had been in Chestnut Hill – she helped him unpack and put things together, and they made great progress working as a team.

Now, they sat on their grand colonnade, drinking wine, enjoying the evening as their children happily played in the giant backyard. On the new grill near them, Adam was cooking some steaks and corn for dinner. They were both very happy to feel that the cool breeze racing along the hilltop was being channeled through the house, making it comfortable and inviting.

Ava finished her glass of wine and poured herself another as Adam saw to the steaks. "OK, I have to admit it," she said, glowing a bit more than normal due to the beverage of choice that evening. "This is wicked awesome."

Adam smiled at her. "Well, I hate to say I told you so, but...I told you so."

She laughed. "You're a big jerk."

"Yeah," he agreed, laughing along with his wife and finishing his wine as well. "I am."

He sat back down next to his wife and kissed her. "OK, but, seriously," Ava said. "This is great. The house is more gorgeous than I ever thought it could be, the grounds are perfect, this view is...what, I can't even..."

"Spectacular?" he offered.

"Yes! *Spectacular*," she said, slurring her words slightly. "I love my job. You obviously are thrilled to be here. I think the kids are happy where they are. This is great." She looked at him lovingly, taking his hand in hers. "I can't wait to see what happens next for us here."

Adam kissed her again and, smiling widely, said. "Neither can I, my dear. Neither can I."

They both turned to watch the kids playing in the large back yard. This was the first time they'd ever lived in a place with a back yard like this, so the kids were having a great time simply running around and being goofy as only a seven-year-old boy and his four-year-old sister can be. Ava watched as they played, taking in the truly spectacular view of the river valley below them, and the touching view of her children playing happily before her.

Adam saw all this too, but he also saw so much more than did everyone else. Right now, he was able to see an Indian, a bloody slash across his half black-painted face that had obliterated his aquiline nose, a tomahawk lodged deep inside his shaved head, standing near the edge of the woods watching. This had been going on since that day in August when the one voice spoke to him convincingly. With every trip back to unload and unpack, he'd seen more and more of the ghosts trapped in this house.

What had first started off as quick glimpses in the corner of his eyes, shadows that seemed to dissipate as soon as he focused on them, Adam now saw them for a moment as fully formed figures before they'd seem to blow away, like smoke in the wind. He'd seen the bloody Indian before. He'd seen whom he knew to be Samuel King, his gray Victorian era suit covered in smears of blood, whispering and laughing to himself. He'd seen a little girl of about Sophie's age, drenched wet, her blanched and water-logged bloated figure standing near the pool simply staring at him with dead white eyes.

This was now Adam's daily life.

But more than these fleeting pictures of lives long ago lost here, he saw *him*. He'd always appear as a thin, pale young man, with long, raven black hair, and a neatly trimmed beard that was equally pitch black. The odor of some peculiar incense, like a sweetly burning spice, ever seemed to surround him like a cloud. He always appeared wearing a formal suit that was often strangely archaic, antiquated, or otherwise unique.

Today, as he stood in a corner of the colonnade, silently watching the kids play and Adam grill the steaks, he was dressed in a long black coat, pin-striped gray pants, a white silk vest buttoned to his neck, a dark red cravat, black leather gloves, and spats on his shiny black boots. Adam saw him everywhere now, always standing silently in a corner of the house, always there, always watching. *Knowing.* His pale gray eyes ever on Adam, observing his every move.

"How's dinner?" Ava said as Adam again flipped the steaks, his attention drawn away from him for a moment. When Adam again looked in the corner, the man was gone.

"Looks like they're about done. You want to gather up the kiddos?"

Ava did so, and they settled down to their first family dinner in the new home. They sat at the table in a dining room still surrounded by half-empty boxes, but that didn't take away from the dinner they had one bit. Adam asked Junior how he liked his new classmates, and he went into a lengthy and circuitous discussion of how much he liked Timmy and Bobbie, both of whom also liked *Star Wars*, but that Timmy liked the old *Star Wars* more than the new and thought Darth Vadar could beat up Kylo Ren wicked easy, but that Bobbie thought that was stupid, and that Bobbie was actually also another Junior, but he didn't go by Junior, so it was OK that there were two Juniors in his class since the teacher called him Adam anyway. He also added that Elsie was nice, for a girl, but that Julie was a meanie and he didn't like her very much.

Adam teased him that when a girl is a meanie to a boy that usually meant she actually liked him, to which Junior responded by making puking sounds.

"That's how it worked for your mother and me," he joked. "She was a meanie to me, too, at our first date, but since I wouldn't go away, she eventually just got used to me."

"*Moooooom!*," Junior wailed. "Is that true?"

"Umm, no," she said, giggling, remembering their first date in a very different way than the one Adam was describing. She smiled hungrily at Adam. "That's not how I remember it at all."

He winked, remembering that night just as well as did she.

Sophie, for her end of things, said that Lizzie and Mel were nice and that she really liked playing with all the new dollies. Adam and Ava were very pleased she seemed to be doing nicely in her pre-school and getting along with all the new kids. Ava talked about settling into her job and the program her team would be developing there as she sipped more wine, complimenting Adam on how good the steak was.

Overall, it was a lovely evening, exactly what both Adam and Ava were hoping for in this move. After dishes and a few more glasses of wine, it was time to get the kids to bed. Two quick baths and then tucking the kids into their beds, which were the only things really squared away in their respective bedrooms. The kids' rooms were next to each other on one wing, while Adam's and Ava's were on the other wing of the house.

The kids tucked in, the wine kicking in, erotic memories of a very satisfying first date coursing through their minds, they turned to each other after closing Sophie's bedroom door, and immediately pounced, flying into each other's arms, kissing passionately. Making their way to their bedroom, which, like the kids' rooms, also only had the bed set up yet, they stripped off their clothes even before making it all the way there.

Their hands roamed each other's body freely, as did their lips and tongues. Although that first date was nearly thirty years ago, and the passion-driven, hormone-crazed young people they were then long ago lost forever, this night it was as if all their youthful aching desires returned with a crash. They explored, they teased, they stroked, licked, and sucked. Once Adam finally got on top and slid into his dripping slick wife, she almost immediately had an orgasm. After her body was done tensing and convulsing, even as Adam continued to pound away at her furiously, she felt another orgasm building, only to explode out a few moments later. Adam continued, jackhammer like, to make love to his wife, and as she felt a third orgasm developing deep inside her, Adam finally let loose a thick torrent into her womb, groaning loudly as he did so. She pulled him tightly to her as he filled her, her legs clasped around him to pull him in even deeper.

After allowing the last dribbled squirts to enter Ava, Adam rolled off his wife, panting, spent, and utterly delighted. "That...that...that was amazing," he said, trying desperately to catch his breath as he covered himself with the sheet.

"Yes, it was," she purred back to him. "I don't know what's gotten into us tonight, but I'm damn certain this was better than even that first date."

"Mmhmmm..." he agreed, his breathing slowly coming back to normal. "You can bet your sweet little ass it was."

Ava reached out to gently stroke Adam's face as he lay there, eyes closed, arms behind his head. As she did, she noticed a curiously shaped object protruding the bedsheet upwards triumphantly. Shocked and yet hungrily amazed at the same time, she diverted her hand downward to confirm

Ava laughed. "I thought you might've been asleep. You must've been dreaming because the whole time you were whispering something."

"Oh, that's too weird. What was I whispering?"

"I don't know, you were mumbling. I, honestly, wasn't paying attention for wonderfully obvious reasons." She smiled and winked at him.

"Oh, myyyyy..." Adam said. "I am such a naughty boy."

"Mhmm..." Ava agreed. "What's really funny is as soon as you were done, you plopped right over and started snoring. Mumbling again."

Adam laughed loudly at that final detail. "Oh, my goodness, are you kidding me?! That's too funny. Like, 'I've done my duty here, ma'am, time to go,' like I'm some kind of sexual cowboy. That's just too damn funny! Could you tell what I was saying?"

Ava thought for a moment, then said, "No, but it sounded like 'and row me to the lake,' over and over until you zonked all the way out." Ava shrugged, and said, "Whatever. Doesn't really matter. All I know is I woke this morning and felt *wonder-fuuuuul*."

She leaned in again, kissing Adam deeply, touching his cheek. She looked at his sturdy craftsman-style desk. "Say, my beast. I don't think we've ever tested out how strong this desk is, have we?"

Adam smiled and was just about to answer that there is no time like the present, when they heard little feet running towards them together with a combined "*Moooooooooooooom!*" from their children. They rolled their eyes at each other, but smiled anyway, now seeing to the needs of their children rather than their own primal needs instead.

[10]

Two weeks later, Adam was lying in bed naked and wide awake, staring at the ceiling of his bedroom and listening to the now perpetual low murmuring of whispers he constantly heard. He slept deliciously that first night, wonderfully drained from the marathon lovemaking with Ava and just generally satisfied with how things were proceeding. Since then, however, with each passing night, the quality of his sleep had declined a little while the buzz in his head from the unending voices increased. When he awoke this night, suddenly pulled out of one of the dark, twisted, and violent nightmares he was now having on a regular basis, he thought he'd heard his own name being whispered. It was difficult for Adam to tell with the constant chatter of voices, which he feared were slowly driving him insane.

But he supposed this was the price one had to pay when chosen to perform a higher duty.

He lay there with his nakedness uncovered due to stifling air in their room, despite the chilly early October night and their wide-open windows. He'd known, of course, that the perceived stuffiness would return after that first night, but that awareness didn't make sleeping in it any easier. Adam lay there, staring at the ceiling and lazily tracing his fingertips along Ava's ass under the sheet covering her. They'd made love that night as well, as they were now more nights than not, and he always had been a big fan of her perfectly contoured bottom.

Adam desperately wanted to go back to sleep, desperately needed to drift off into what he hoped would be a dream-free, blissfully recuperative experience – yet there was another part of him that now feared to fall asleep. In addition to the viciously violent nightmares haunting his sleep, Adam had started sleepwalking throughout his house and the grounds outside. He'd awoken once standing in complete darkness on the cold brick of the basement, one time outside next to the pool freezing in the cold autumn air, and on several occasions in the kids' doorways, staring at them with sleep vacant eyes.

Of all these odd sleepwalking destinations, that was the most concerning to him, because he'd be humiliated – and the kids terrified – if they were to wake with him standing there nude, staring at them in the dead of the night. Though they were raising the kids to be body positive and comfortable with their own nudity, waking to find their father standing speechless in their doorway wearing no clothes would be a bit much for the little ones.

As Adam lay there, the odor of a faraway wood fire now wafted into his room, together with what smelled like burnt meat. He thought this odd because the air outside was as still as it was inside his listless room. Adam wondered if there were overnight campers at the nearby state reservation and thought it interesting that he could smell their ruined dinner. But even as he thought on this curiosity, he realized he could hear an unusual soft dragging sound coming from the balcony outside his room.

He sat up, straining his ears to make the strange sounds

out more clearly. He heard at first a loud clunk, followed by the dragging sound, followed by another clunk. Dragging sound...clunk. Dragging sound...clunk. Dragging sound...clunk. The sounds were rhythmic and regular, proceeding at a steady pace and seeming to now be going down the steps.

Adam leaped out of bed, feeling compelled to find out where the sounds are coming from, though there was a part of him that already knew exactly what was happening. He had neither fear nor trepidation about what might be waiting for him out there, no more so than does another homeowner when figuring out why a board in their floor creaks. The knowingness he'd developed since that hot day in August had allowed him to perceive so much of what was going on in his house, and to approach each newly revealed secret with anticipation and excitement.

He walked softly to the balcony, and there in the dim light, he saw Samuel King dragging the naked body of his daughter, Elizabeth, down the stairs. His suit was smeared with blood, his face covered in a frenzy of red spatters. Elizabeth's head had been pounded so many times with a heavy ax that the only remaining discernable features were her chin and lower teeth, and one, wide-open glazed eye staring out into the dark. Everything else was a smashed and ruined bloody mash of what used to be a human head.

Adam looked, and saw her long, brown, blood-soaked hair was leaving a red trail of smears coming from what was now Junior's room.

As the ghost of Samuel King slowly dragged his dead daughter's body down the stairs, making her head bounce sickly off each step, he whispered and laughed softly to himself. Adam watched, unable to make out what he was saying, but also unable to look away from this macabre scene.

Halfway down the steps, King suddenly stopped whispering, and slowly lifted his eyes to meet Adam's. He nodded his head once and smiled, then whispered, "Welcome." He then returned to whispering inanely and giggling as he dragged his dead daughter down the steps.

Drag...clunk! Drag...clunk! Drag...clunk!

Adam stood there watching as King dragged her all the way down the stairs, then slowly made his way along the foyer to what was now the dining room, the blood trail staining the white marble blocks a pinkish hue. Curious to see how this sad story ended, Adam walked down the stairs as well, feeling Elizabeth's thick warm blood against his bare feet as he did, oozing between his toes. He followed the trail into the dark dining room, then turned on the light to see nothing but their dining table and buffet.

He furrowed his brow, glancing behind him to see the long bloody trail had completely disappeared. As he did, Adam again smelled the wood fire and burnt meat odor, only now overwhelmingly powerful. He lifted his eyes to see the figure of a man who was burnt to a black crisp standing in the foyer, silently staring at him.

This man was burnt to the bone, so looked more like a skeleton covered in a thin wrapping of black and curled crispy skin. His nose was burned away, revealing a skull's gaping opening in the center of his face instead, and though some charred skin still clung to his face around his cheeks, the man's lips were utterly destroyed, peeled away to make it appear as if he were madly smiling a toothy grin at Adam. Smoke rose lazily from the man, and he seemed to sizzle beneath his still-pristine clothing. Though no historical expert, Adam judged the clothing to be from sometime in the 1600s given how outlandish and fancy it was. Despite being burned to a blackened mass of destroyed skin, the man's bright green eyes were perfectly preserved in his lidless sockets and now stared ceaselessly into Adam's.

The two simply stood there, staring at each other for a

time, until the burnt man slowly turned, his flesh making rasping, crackling, creaking sounds as he moved. He slowly walked towards the open cellar door, and Adam felt compelled to follow.

He watched as the burnt man slowly descended into the cellar, being swallowed up by the inky blackness. Adam flicked the light switch, but to no avail. The basement remained shrouded in darkness, even as he could still hear the burnt man's raspy walk going down the hallway. Noting the slightest soft glow coming from what seemed to be the rear room, Adam slowly worked his way down the dark steps until he felt the brick floor of the cellar.

Smelling the odor of fire but now no longer seeing the burnt man, Adam saw the soft glow of candlelight coming from the room at the end of the hall. He proceeded down the hallway, passing the closed door of every storage room until he finally arrived at the back room, whose door stood slightly ajar, allowing the bright candlelight to pour forth.

He pushed open the door as it made a loud creak to find the room transformed. The brick walls were now covered in bright red drapes, tall iron candelabras in each corner with numerous black candles burning. The rough stone table now looked more like an altar than ever, as four long black candles burned in each corner, while five smaller black votives were arranged in the center around an antique dagger.

Adam slowly walked into the room, the flames from the many candles in the room feeling hot against his naked flesh. He felt drawn towards the dagger on the stone altar, approaching it with reverence and awe, mesmerized by it somehow, yet fearful to reach out and touch it. The candlelight danced against the dull gray of the blade, pulling him in closer and closer. It was as if the ancient blade itself were speaking to him.

As he stopped just in front of the altar, staring at the old dagger, he smelled the odor of sweet spices even as he heard "Take it," whispered softly from behind him, the air becoming unbearably stifling and listless. Tensing suddenly, he turned cautiously to see the pale young man, dressed in a tight-fitting red suit with long tails, a black shirt, and a modern black tie under his red vest. He crept closer and closer to Adam, standing now beside him. Extending a gloved hand and pointing at the dagger, he again ordered, "Take it" in a more demanding whisper.

Adam reached out to take the dagger, and as he touched it, he could feel it vibrating in his hand, seeming almost to hum with some dark, dread power. He looked at it carefully, seeing that the curved, gilded cross guards and corroded wire-wrapped black leather hilt were dull with age, but even though the blade had small pits and pot marks from the many years, still it was razor-sharp. The round, dirty gilt pommel was dented slightly as if having been used to pound something in the long distant past.

As Adam looked at the blade, he noted that near the hilt it was roughly etched with the same design he'd seen all those months ago when they'd first visited Cromwell's Ferry. He gently rubbed the design with his thumb. Then, it was nothing but a meaningless abstract shape to him, but now he had learned the awesome potential behind this sigil. Knowing now the meaning and use of this strange shape, he whispered the name it represented with deep devotion in his voice.

"Andromelech," he said. The pale young man smiled broadly, his fanged teeth protruding as he did so.

Adam took the dagger fully in his hand, wrapping his fingers more completely around the hilt, liking the vibrating sense of power. It was as if he were committing himself to use the dagger the way it was intended to be. He turned it in his hand, holding it as a fighter would if they wanted to stab someone repeatedly with a barrage of downward blows. It felt right, it felt comfortable, it felt powerful. Most importantly, it felt *good* for Adam to hold the dagger like that.

Adam looked at Andromelech, seeing the demon's pale gray eyes boring into his own, the fanged smile on his face growing with evil anticipation. Adam was just about to ask a question when Andromelech whispered, "Man...you will know what to do."

He then snapped his gloved fingers.

Adam instantly found himself standing in his bedroom, his right arm raised high above his head, his fist clenched as if holding something, but his hand empty. He was standing next to his bed, his raised fist hovering over his sleeping wife as if he'd intended to pummel Ava in her sleep. It was many hours later, the sky turning bright pink as the sun began to peek over the horizon. Despite the stifling air, Adam was cold from having been standing there nude for so many hours. His joints ached, especially his right shoulder and hand.

Adam slowly and painfully made his way to his side of the bed, every muscle in his body stiff, achy, and sore from having been in that awkward position for so long. His feet throbbed from having stood for so many hours. He got in bed and happily covered up with the sheet and down quilt, feeling a chill that seems to have seeped deep inside his body. As he lay there, sleep quickly beginning to overtake him, he wondered if that bizarre event even happened at all, or did he dream the whole thing while once again sleepwalking. As he fell asleep, he couldn't tell whether it had been a fantasy or a waking reality.

A few hours later, Adam awoke after enjoying a pleasantly deep slumber, grateful for a brief respite of nightmare-free sleep. He reached out to feel for Ava, but her side of the bed was both empty and cold. He looked around, remembering that bizarre overnight...what was it, Adam wondered. Event?

Vision? Sleep-walking dream? He couldn't at that moment tell.

Adam got dressed and went downstairs, finding Ava in the kitchen making Sunday morning brunch, the kids already eating. They kissed and she smiled at him, the way she always did on a morning following deeply satisfying sex.

"How are things this morning?" he asked Ava.

"Well, I'm terrific, but these two are little crank pots," she said. She explained that both had been up early and generally whiny this morning over nothing specific. They were both just in foul moods, and miserable as a result.

"So, guess who's getting naps early today?" Ava asked, eliciting even more whining from the pair. "I can't imagine what's gotten into them. Can you?"

Adam stood at the kitchen sink getting himself some water, looking out on their lawn. There he saw three small naked children huddling together for warmth, their hair whipping wildly in an unseen blizzard, their skin a frozen bluish-white. They looked at Adam, imploring him to somehow end their misery.

"Nope," he said, answering Ava's question as he stared blankly at the ghosts of those long-dead children before they dissipated and blew away. "I have no idea."

He joined his family at the kitchen table, drinking his coffee and trying to participate in the rambling morning dialog, but he was entirely too distracted by wondering about what had happened the previous night.

After dishes he told Ava he planned to work on the book in his study, but on the way stopped at the cellar stairs first. He flicked the light switch, and the lights dutifully illuminated the basement as he expected. He went down, looked all around, and once again found nothing out of the ordinary. He walked into the rear room, where he found everything exactly as he expected. No red drapes, no candelabras, no dagger. Everything looked perfectly normal.

Yet despite the appearance of normalcy, he knew at that moment everything he recalled from last night had happened exactly as he remembered it; as he stood there looking at the dull stone table, Adam smelled an overwhelming odor of burnt flesh and heard the rasping of crispy skin moving slightly in the dark behind him.

THE WINDS RATTLED THE WINDOWS AND MADE THE EAVES creak that night, even as Ava's heart rattled in her chest.

She sat in her bathroom on that windy Halloween night staring incredulously at the very clear indicator on her home pregnancy test. Two lines. Two unmistakably pink lines. There was simply no misinterpreting that; even if there was, she'd had the foresight to get two, and it was the second one she now stared at, slack-jawed, shocked.

"Oh, my..." she whispered, her heart still excitedly thrumming inside her. "Oh, boy. Oh...my-my-my,"

Living atop an otherwise unoccupied hill near an abandoned ghost town is hardly a good set up for a fun Halloween for small children, so Ava took the kids into Deerfield with some new work friends of hers so they could go trick-or-treating like usual and enjoy the night. Though a bit more inconvenient than walking the kids around their Chestnut Hill neighborhoods, meeting her work crew in Deerfield to take the kids around there was a reasonable option.

As the winds began to blow through the old streets of

Deerfield, making this already chilly night with low-hanging mists and a bright full moon feel even more like a perfect Halloween, Ava's co-worker, Ruth, said to her, "I'm going to have to stay away from the kids' candy, because I'm about to get my period. I'm liable to eat all of it before they got any." Ava at first merely laughed at this, thinking about her own monthly ravenous behavior when it suddenly occurred to her she was late.

Her periods had been more irregular and lighter since giving birth to Sophie four years earlier, so she hadn't been as acutely aware of the timing as she had been earlier in her life. Her anticipated date for this month came and went without her realizing it, and it wasn't until Ruth mentioned her own impending period that she'd even thought of it.

Once the thought had entered her mind, however, Ava found it hard to let it go. She knew it could just be a missed month, as she'd had many times before, or it could just as easily come tomorrow or the next day. However, something about this just *felt* like it could be far more than simply a missed period.

She found it hard to focus on the kids' and their happy chatter, hearing Junior but not really responding when he said he thought they had mice in the attic because of the scratching noises he heard up there at night, and merely nodding when Sophie added that Mel says there are scary things in her attic. She marched along with the Halloween crew, present but not truly there at all as her mind raced with the possibilities.

So, when at one point in their trick-or-treating the pack of babbling children and parents passed a drug store, she slipped in for a moment to buy herself the pregnancy tests.

"Oh, my," she said again. "Oh, dear. Oh...boy, oh boy."

Ava stood, her hands going naturally to touch her belly, though it was far too early for anything even approaching a bump to have developed in the womb beneath her hands. Nonetheless, she gently touched where a small life had unexpectedly taken root inside her and had recently started to grow, a process she had always found nothing short of miraculous.

A miraculous process that was always inevitably terrifying for Ava. Though she loved children desperately and had dedicated her entire career to their welfare, and though the role she identified with most fully was that of mother, she still found the process of having a small human growing inside of her, a life for which she was personally responsible, to be thoroughly frightening. This was even when she was fully prepared and the baby planned for.

That was not currently the case. She and Adam had agreed that two kids – especially the "million-dollar family" of one boy and one girl – was enough for them, and since then Ava had been taking her birth control pills regularly. She'd sadly accepted that Sophie would be her last, knowing Adam had already sacrificed a lot of his wishes to have the two they'd had, and so Ava had simply figured she'd allow time and menopause to do the inevitable. But life, which in her view was the ultimate trickster, now threw a fast one at her she never saw coming. So, now she had added to the stress of pregnancy the extra feature of it being totally unexpected.

But, hey, unexpected things are part of the joy of life, right? Right?!

Ava's mind wandered now, wondering how Adam would react to the pregnancy. She knew full well he felt some resentment when Junior was born due to all the time she'd had to devote to the baby and because of how their son's presence changed the lifestyle they'd enjoyed up to that point. She suspected Adam still had some level of antipathy for him, given how quick he was to criticize Junior's annoying behaviors, how harsh Adam could sometimes be correcting him, yet then have endless patience for Sophie's meltdowns. Ava likewise knew he would have been happy going through life without having any kids at all. She worried suddenly about how he would react to this wildly unanticipated news.

Ava desperately wanted Adam to be as thrilled as she was, a thrill she was able to feel now that the shock was wearing off, but feared he wouldn't be. He'd always been such a vocal advocate for abortion, Ava worried he might ask her to get one, perhaps even pressure her to do so. Even though she supported the right to choose, Ava knew she could never bring herself to willingly abort her baby, this almost magical creation growing inside of her, right under her heart, that she and Adam created in an act of love.

So, Ava thought, *I'm going to exercise my right to choose by choosing to have this baby, even though Adam might not like that. He'll just have to learn to love bambino number three, is all.* Ava again rubbed her non-existent bump.

She knew one thing Adam was likely to say was that he's entirely too old to have another child, that he wasn't up to the challenge, that he was too set in his ways for bottles and diapers and all that all over again. That was a legitimate concern, she had to admit, one that had crossed her mind earlier. Adam was 51 years old, which means he'd be 64 when the baby hit the teen years and 71 when their child turned 20. Counterposed against this basic math, Ava reminded herself, was that Adam remained in great shape for a man of any age, ate very healthfully, and took very good care of his health. There'd be no reason to believe he wouldn't be able to keep up with a baby.

But what about you? Aren't you too old?

"Ah, yes," Ava said to herself in answer to her own thoughts. "There's the voice of my perpetual doubt and insecurity."

Ava looked at herself in the mirror. She looked hard, not

merely looking at herself but *into* herself, sizing up her ability to manage this unintended joy and tremendous duty. Her tightly curled brown hair had some streaks of gray, but not many. Her build was fit and strong, her coffee-colored skin looked fresh, and, perhaps most importantly, she *felt* empowered, competent, and confident. After some minutes, she felt fully convinced that not only did she look better than some women half her 48 years, but that she had all the energy, vim, and vigor needed to manage the demands of a new baby regardless of her age. She knew a pregnancy at this age, regardless of the mother's optimistic disposition, was always tricky, but she felt fully up to this.

"I'm going to mother the shit out of this," she said to her own reflection, feeling powerful and ready to have the discussion with Adam.

Ava found him in his study, where seemed to be almost exclusively these days, typing at his computer from notes written on his legal pad. She walked in and realized suddenly how very tired he looked, remembering then how obsessed with work he'd become when writing his first book, too.

"Hey, you," she said, kissing him on the head as he continued to type.

"Hey yourself. Do you think the kids have diabetes yet?" he asked. Junior and Sophie had dumped out their plastic pumpkin containers full of candy on the floor just outside his study, so he said how entertained he'd been hearing them sift through their haul to get the good pieces – and eat them right away, of course. "They're like little archeologists going through an ancient treasure trove. Very cute."

Ava chuckled. "Yeah, that they sure are. How's the book going?"

"Oh, great," Adam answered distractedly, not stopping his typing as he spoke. "No one will believe some of this stuff I've dug up. This is going to be huge. Unfortunately, I'm obviously going to miss the election, but *c'est la vie*. It's coming very nicely, but I'd forgotten how hooked on this I get when I write. I need to push away from the desk more often, go for a run or something."

"Yes!" Ava agreed, perhaps too excitedly. "That's an excellent, really superb idea. You've *got* to take care of yourself."

Adam stopped to look at her oddly for a moment, then continued to type.

She closed the door over so the kids couldn't hear their conversation as well. "So, do you remember our first night here?"

Adam stopped typing again to look Ava in the eyes, smiling. "Remember it? I'll never forget it. It's the thing fantasies are made of."

"Well, apparently something happened that night, something...uh...unplanned."

He looked at her now even more intently, blanching somewhat. "What...what happened?"

Ava took a deep breath. "Well...I'm pregnant," she said with a shrug. "You got me pregnant that night."

Here it comes.

Adam continued to stare at her, mouth hanging open stupidly, until he suddenly stood and raced to her, hugging her fiercely. "This is wonderful news! Oh, I'm so thrilled!" he said, so loudly the kids fell into silence as they stopped their sifting for a moment, only to get distracted by some fun-sized Snickers. "I'm so happy, Ava!"

Adam kissed her, smiling broadly when they pulled apart as she looked at him with confusion.

"What?" he said when he saw her look.

"I just didn't...this isn't the...I'm just..." Ava stammered, unable to find the right words as her mind raced with complete surprise. "I'm sorry, this isn't the reaction I was expecting. Not at all. Don't get me wrong, I'm very happy with this reaction, it's just not what I expected."

"What'd you expect?"

"Well, to be honest, I thought you'd be upset. We'd agreed to only have two kids, you'd said in counseling that the transition of becoming a parent was difficult, we just moved in here and have only now gotten settled in, things are still weird at work for you, you're in the middle of a book...I thought you might even think yourself too old."

"Old?" Adam said, smiling incredulously. "Are you calling me old?"

"No, I'm not...you're just, you know..."

"Old?"

"Yeah, kind of."

Adam pulled Ava to him and kissed her forehead, saying, "It's a good thing I love you, you brat." After pulling apart, he said, "All those concerns were valid, I'll admit it. But I've felt so different since we've moved in here, we've had so much time together as a family, the pace is so much slower and things just feel more...I don't know, relaxed? Everything you mentioned entered my mind, but then I just opened myself up to what was going to be, you know?"

"Yeah, I do," Ava said, still surprised by Adam's reaction. "I get that."

"I guess there are some things bigger than we are, and there's no use fighting."

"OK then. Awesome," Ava said, thrilled and relieved by this conversation.

Junior and Sophie joined them in the study not long after that, still in their Mandalorian and Rey costumes, to show off their favorite pieces of candy from the night. As they bustled about the study on a sugar high, Ava and Adam had some further discussions about how they plan to keep up with the demands of a newborn – and, in a few years, an even more demanding toddler – what they need to do to get ready to have a baby in the house all over again, when to tell the kids and then the various family members, and even a few early name suggestions. They hugged, feeling very comfortable and contended with this curveball to their lives.

Ava took the kids out to get baths and ready for bed, Adam saying he'd be up as soon as he finished the chapter he was working on. She thought about how surprised yet grateful she was for Adam's wonderful reaction to this news, as well as a whole host of other details.

As she bathed then kids, who by then were again cranky and clearly in need of sleep, joined then by Adam to help get them to bed, Ava realized how exhausted she felt. Her emotions had been all over the place this evening, from the first she realized that she'd missed her period, to confirming her suspicions with the pregnancy tests, to her fears of Adam's reaction and then, finally, his very different response. She now felt contented, with the sudden letting out of all that emotion leaving her feeling like a happily deflated ragdoll.

Overall, Ava felt very certain this was one Halloween night she would long remember.

[12]

As one of the most brutal winters Massachusetts had seen in decades descended on them not long after the new year, as the winds blew wickedly and the snows piled up around them, Adam worked hard to maintain his sanity. That long, viciously cold winter passed with agonizing slowness, an agony that was entirely shared in Adam's personal struggle.

As far as anyone in the family could tell he was merely tired and overworked, spending hours in his study working feverishly on his book about the impeachment. Ava had noted he was quiet and looked pale, a little thinner, with circles under his eyes, but she assumed it was only because of his intense work schedule. Adam had acted and looked the same way when he wrote his first book, so she had no real reason for concern. When he broke away from his desk at the end of his workday to spend time with the family, he appeared to be playful, jovial, and everything Ava loved about her husband – though that was largely a performance not entirely of his enacting. To Ava, he just seemed deeply fatigued, tired to his very core.

But Adam knew the truth.

He had been able to hear the never-ending chorus of whispering constantly since just after moving in, but the volume and intensity of these whispers had been gradually growing over the weeks. Their constant chatter was making it difficult for him to think clearly, certainly difficult to focus on what his family was saying to him. Worse than the demanding intensity of the voices for Adam was that he could now clearly hear the specific words being whispered. He was able to make out of the cacophony individual voices, distinct whispers, not in long or consistent threads, but rather in small spurts. Since he could now hear the voices, Adam could also make out the foul and vile things being said to him.

"They're all going to die, Adam," the voices would often whisper to him. *"We're going to eat their souls and feast on their flesh..."*

The voices were like a constantly pounding drum hammering inside his own head. He tried to ignore them, but to no avail; they were too powerful. He begged them to stop, but uselessly; they were too altogether evil. He cried, exhausted and defeated; they laughed at him, tormenting him, delighting in his suffering.

"Go away," he would whisper into the long, dark night of his bedroom, tortured, tired and alone, as the rest of his family slept dreamlessly. He'd sit awake in his bed on the verge of tears, pushing his fists into his forehead, almost as if to prevent his head from splitting open, begging for succor. "Leave me alone, please. I'll do it, I said I would do it, just please stop. Go away."

The voices didn't care, nor did they ever depart.

"We're here, Adam, and we want you all to stay with us..."

Adam was now scarcely sleeping because of the relentless jabbering of the voices and their cruel taunting, and when he did, his slumber was polluted by dreams of such horrific violence that he'd often have to bury his face in a pillow to quiet his screams, as he didn't want to wake up Ava. While before he might have only seen snippets of the gruesome violence that had taken place on this hill, he was now being dragged through it, event after event after bloody event, in mind-numbing detail.

Adam came to understand through his torturous nightmares that the demon called Andromelech had possessed many different places over hundreds of centuries, and everywhere he went he brought destruction, death, and torment with him (something, Dear Friend, you will come to realize is a common practice amongst demons of his rank). He'd claimed this area as his own for tens of thousands of years and this hill had long been an epicenter of evil.

During these long, seemingly endless cold winter nights, Adam would be forced to repeatedly watch every act of maniacal violence that ever happened on this spot. As the bitter winds howled outside the window, he'd be made to watch women get raped and then gutted, babies impaled on stakes simply for cruel pleasure, and men slowly skinned alive to prolong their nightmarish torment. As the sleet and hail beat against their slate roof, Adam would have to hear the shrieks of captured tribal enemies as they were burned as sacrifices, or the sound of bones slowly cracking in torture, then, once dead, of being snapped open to allow fresh, still-warm marrow to be sucked out.

Adam would wake suddenly in his sleep, sitting up with ravening, bulging eyes, shocked by the mad terror of his dreams, slick with sweat, stifling his screams as his heart pounded in his chest. The sounds he'd been forced to hear would echo in his head as they faded to the wind whistling outside, the images, like a slowly fading flash burn, would melt to the inky black of his dark bedroom. Then he'd lay staring at the ceiling, sleepless, as the voices took over his ceaseless torment.

"They laughed at you then, Adam. They're laughing at you now..."

If Adam should happen to fall back to sleep, then the panoply of historical torments would continue, from the earliest days of the demon's occupation many thousands of years ago up to the present age. Night after night of impenetrable winter darkness, of icy cold bleakness, he'd be punished with ongoing nightmares of the most impossible carnage imaginable.

"Kill them, Adam. Make them pay..."

Adam had also begun sleepwalking with greater frequency as the long winter dragged on, adding to his misery. Several times every week he would find himself waking, often shaking due to the cold despite the still, stuffy air, having been standing in some exposed position for hours. Adam woke once standing in the corner of the cellar colonial kitchen, holding the poker that went to the fireplace down there, whispering unknown words to himself as he did. He awoke once in the attic, standing in what was at one time a servant's room, and several times in his study, staring at the computer screen. Once, Adam painfully awoke from a sleepwalk standing on the colonnade as a wicked winter wind blew and howled, ice pelting off his naked skin. He had luckily left the rear doors open, or else he might have been locked out and frozen to death on his own back porch.

Often, though, Adam had awakened from a sleepwalk to find himself holding the dagger. He would never have any recollection of getting it and would never know from where it came, yet he would awaken, standing with the dagger downward pointed in his hand, as if ready to strike and kill. As much as the dagger's appearance in his hand was a mystery to Adam, so to was the fact that, regardless of where he placed it when he returned to his bed, he would wake in the morning to find it gone.

"Kill them..."

Most horrifying, though, was the night Adam realized his nightmares and his sleepwalking were overlapping, and that he was having trouble separating dreams and fantasies from reality. His nightmares, though typically long vignettes of the violence that had occurred on this spot over the years, had started to become increasingly personal. Adam was dreaming, more and more, of committing acts of horrible violence against his own family members. These he found particularly horrific, the difference between witnessing violence committed against an unknown person compared to a loved one being significant.

He dreamt that night that he was murdering his son, stabbing Junior in the back repeatedly as the boy slept peacefully on his belly. Even as Adam dreamt this horrible scene, there was a still a part of him fully aware of the horror of it, and that part screamed out silently for him to stop this evil, yet in his dream, he'd raise the dagger up and slam it down into his son's back with a wet *thwock!* as it sliced through skin, cut into bone and spinal cord, piercing lung and heart repetitively. In his nightmare, Adam repeated this murderous action until Junior's torso was nothing but a bloody wreck.

The terror of Adam's dream became even more palpable when he awoke, sleepwalking in Junior's doorway, holding the dagger in his hand. His son lay exactly as he had seen him in his nightmare, arms tucked under his pillow supporting his head, on his belly, back fully exposed. When he looked and saw he was holding the dagger, Adam sucked in his breath in abject fear, quickly backing out of Junior's bedroom and stumbling backward, falling as he dropped the dagger. He pushed himself back from the dagger as he realized how close he came to potentially killing his own son, weeping bitter tears and groaning as he implored, "No, no, no! You can't make me do this. You can't. Not this. *Not this!*"

As the weeks of torment turned into months of pain, signs of inevitable spring sluggishly started to show outside. The nights were slowly getting shorter and shorter, and while earlier sunrises might potentially feel to Adam like a savior arriving to ease his suffering, the sunlight conceivably feeling like a salve against Adam's anguish – nothing really changed. The slight warming breezes that now blew from the south, the occasional rains that now fell rather than the oppressive snows, seemed like a calming balm – but with no difference in Adam's now twisted life. New, fresh, green life started to grow outside, bringing with it the annual promise of hope – but Adam kept none for himself.

At the beginning of each day he felt pummeled, beaten by his own anguished dreams, only to find the days filled with their own sufferings.

He was lost, and he knew it.

"Kill them all..."

Adam had no recourse in the daylight, no true relief to look forward to with the rising of the sun. What was the sun to Adam? Nothing but a far distant source of light, an out-of-reach place of warmth. It might mean the end of a terror to many, maybe the sign of hope for some, perhaps representing the promise of a new era, but not to him. He was trapped here, on Earth, in this house on a hill, his own pocket of horror. The sun meant nothing to him now.

The nightmares he was having were no longer restricted to his sleeping hours. More and more often with his waking eyes, Adam saw the violent history of this house played out before him. Just as his nightmares gave him a detailed tour of the violent past of this hill, in his waking visions Adam was compelled to view the long, horrible past of his home. Yet as horrendous as his nightmares were, they paled in comparison after time to these waking fantasies. Horrific as were the images of the violence in his home at first, images that grew daily in intensity and disgust, these had recently begun to focus on the equally long history of sexual violence that had occurred in the house.

"Your mother fucked men in your house when you were a little boy, and your father knew, but was too much of a weak-willed pussy to stop her..."

He'd only been shown glimpses of the sexual violence here previously, but now he was being forced to view it in completely unrestricted, unsettling clarity.

Uzziah Blackstone, in addition to being the first settler in the area, was also the first slave owner and trader as his mercantile enterprise grew. Uzziah would often descend into the original cellar of the home, all the kitchen slaves stopping their work, eyes cast down to the floor, as an icy cold panic would steal over their bodies, goosebumps dancing over their skin as fear leaped through them. He would pace slowly in the kitchen, arms behind his back, inspecting his female slaves as he did when he first bought them in the Boston slave markets. Calmly and slowly would he scrutinize them, until suddenly striking like a coiled snake, he would clutch a young slave girl by her throat and drag her to one of the storage rooms as she screamed, begging for help, pleading for mercy. There was none to be found.

All the other kitchen slaves would quickly return to their work as they tried desperately to ignore the sounds coming from the storage room, the sounds of the slave girl screaming, of being punched and slapped, of bones cracking, of her being whipped and choked, of flesh slapping harshly against flesh. They all knew full well what was happening in that room, having all been Uzziah's target at one point in time. However long the torment lasted, whenever it finally ended, they would come out of the room together, Uzziah disheveled, red-faced and panting, dragging the bleeding slave girl behind him as she walked limping, wracked with pain, with puffy, bruised eyes and broken teeth.

Uzziah particularly liked to buy young, nubile female slaves as house servants he'd direct to be used for cleaning only his bedroom, closet, and study. These girls he would initially treat especially well, giving them pieces of fresh fruit, silk ribbons, and other small baubles as a sign of being his favorite.

He would, in time, tell these slave girls there was something in a private outbuilding, built far from the others, that he wanted to share only with them because they were his special favorite. There, Uzziah would delight in blindfolding the girls, playing a game with them in which they had to wander around trying to find him to claim a prize. They would blunder about in the vacant space, believing there was actually some lovely treat waiting for them as they'd been told, when instead he'd suddenly seize them from the rear, forcing their wrists into a pair of shackles behind their backs. This he'd then connect to a strappado he had pending from the ceiling, yanking their arms painfully behind them and upwards, forcing the girls to bend over to stop the anguish in their shoulders. As they shrieked in pain, surprise, and fear, Uzziah would stuff linen rags in their mouths, rip off their clothes, and then shackle their ankles to eyehooks he had secured in the brick floor.

Then, their tortures would begin in earnest, torment which lasted for many long days. Raping the girls time and time again, he would also take great perverse pleasure in slowly removing fingernails, slicing off long strips of skin, pulling out teeth, and doing every other demented, perverted thing imaginable to torture another human being. Watching for the signs, he would continue until the girls were close to death, then, raping them one final time, he would slit their throats even as he filled their wombs with his seed once again.

"She likes it up the ass, Adam. Your mother is a whore. She's a slut..."

This was merely the first detailed story Adam had been forced to watch in the long, gut-wrenching, horrifying history of sexual violence in his home. It seemed every owner of the house had sexually abused their servants, or their children, or both, and Adam was being shown these disturbing images with no hope of ever averting his eyes. Even when Adam was able to break away with a scream and an overt act of extreme will, when he was able to busy himself doing some other task, a trance-like state would eventually descend upon him, and into the pit of these dark images he again would fall.

He was trapped. Most of the time, Adam would sit, immobile, staring blankly, watching vision after vision of sexual violence play out before him as he'd beg in a harsh whisper, "Stop...stop...please stop. I can't take anymore." His begging would illicit only cruel laughter and teasing.

He hated it, yet there was no turning away from it now.

More than just the imagery, however, Adam hated his reaction to it. He'd be compelled to watch these terrible images of sexual violence, images that horrified and disgusted him – yet they had also started to arouse him. Adam had never before enjoyed rough sex, had never been controlling or dominant in the bedroom, and had always been revolted by anything that even approached sexual violence, yet these barrages of horrifying images were arousing him nonetheless, making his cock throb painfully in his pants.

As much as Adam loathed his arousal, he detested this reaction to it even more. At first, Adam would resolutely ignore his cock, pretending it wasn't yearning for release, aching to be unleashed. In time he'd take it out and stroke gently, but not to climax. Now he stroked it with abandon, often drying himself out by the end of the day by having so many thunderous orgasms. Adam hated himself for it but felt almost addicted to the visions.

You're a worthless piece of shit. You'll always be worthless...

Yet despite all this, despite the gnawing fatigue, despite the constant distraction, Adam's book was being written. There was information being documented in his book for the first time that he knew was groundbreaking, secrets that would blow official Washington to pieces. When not being forced to watch scenes of violence, Adam was allowed to envision himself basking in the glow of having revealed numerous secrets, of having ruined the political careers of some of the people he most desperately loathed, of watching as they scurried like insects from the light he shone under their filthy rocks. He could see himself granting interviews and becoming a media darling, the same media that had just so recently scoffed at his professionalism, questioned his motivations, demeaned his ethics.

Adam would graciously guide these lesser journalists through his process, subtly reminding them of his inherent superiority. He would have his revenge on the industry that had turned its back on him for doing the right thing, and indeed, on all the people over the years who'd ever belittled or insulted him. His massive fame and fortune, his chance for once to be the news rather than reporting it, Adam believed, would be a delicious vengeance.

Perhaps the best part for Adam about all these rich benefits he would soon reap is that *he* wasn't literally writing the book at all. Adam would go to his computer dutifully every morning, log on as normal, open Word, then drift off into another maelstrom of violent images as the words appeared on his blank document as if being dictated by some unseen speaker (which, Dear Friend, they essentially were).

When released from that day's course of shocking images, Adam would note with pleasure that some 20 brilliantly worded pages of new copy had been created in his book, pages that reveal one scathing secret after another.

Which is why, despite his torment, regardless of his suffering, Adam was willing to go through this process. He would become wealthier and famous and powerful, and have his revenge on everyone, whether it was the management of the network, the editorial board of *A New Day*, all the commentators in the industry who'd run his name through the mud after the Epstein revelations, even the mindless hicks from his childhood who tormented him. *Everyone.*

All he must do is pay one small price, and all this fame, fortune, and revenge would be his. Just one, small, irrelevant sacrifice.

"Kill them, Adam. Kill them all…"

The voices had recently become more demanding, insisting Adam harm his family members. His nightmares increasingly showed him just that, in typically gruesome detail. All the long years of violence that had occurred in this house, all the specific acts of pain and torment and torture enacted on others, Adam now saw himself doing to his family night after night. The voices mocked him with this, urging him on.

"Smash her head against the wall, you little pussy. Shove a knife right through his eyes into his brain, Adam…"

But he would fight their demands. Adam had resolved not to give in to the pressure of these wretchedly evil voices. He'd agreed to make a sacrifice in order to appease Andromelech, but he told himself he wouldn't inflict pain on his family, no matter how much the voices tormented him. Though a laborious struggle, and though he was able to tell that more and more of his will was being taken over by the demon to serve only his will, he wouldn't harm his family.

"Douse her with gas while she sleeps and burn the cunt alive..."

As the first day of spring dawned that year, fresh and green and glowing with the promise of new life and rebirth, Adam feared he might be losing his battle to maintain his frayed sanity.

[13]

ON THAT SAME SPRING EQUINOX DAY, AS ADAM SAT IN HIS study on the left-wing of the manor house fighting his own final descent into madness, Ava sat reading a book in her office as she listened to Sophie coloring and jabbering happily to herself in the adjacent room.

She sat gently rocking in a chair that would soon see her soothing her second son, Seth, back to sleep as she fed him from her breasts. Ava had fed all her children in this manner and she had no intention of stopping for baby number three just because she was a bit older. But for now, Ava merely sat there happily reading on this bright and sunny day, slowly rocking in her chair as she rubbed the significant bulge in her belly. From where Ava sat, she could hear Junior watching a Netflix show in his iPad, hear Sophie coloring and talking to herself in the next room, all as she softly rubbed her yet unborn baby. She was happy and very fulfilled.

Things had been going quite well for her personally and for the family in general, and now that the horrible winter they'd all had to suffer through seemed to finally be over she felt even more enthusiastic about the bright future. Ava knew how hard Adam was working on his book, and having read some of the things he'd been able to dig up, she was looking forward to what the critical reaction to his work would be. She personally felt like it had better be ecstatic because she knew how hard he'd been working to get it done, how exhausted Adam was because of writing so many pages of deliciously-worded prose every single day, and all the research he'd put into it by this point. She'd never been prouder and more impressed by Adam in all the years she knew him.

Sophie's loud giggles intruded on her reveries at that moment, as she also said something in that high-pitched, little girl voice of hers that Ava wasn't quite able to make out. Whatever it was she said, Ava thought her daughter sounded darling in there playing by herself, and her heart melted.

Though Ava was so very proud of Adam's work, she was also quite worried about him. She recalled how focused he'd been when he wrote his first book, but this time around he seemed somehow – *different* was the only word she could find to describe it. He looked pale and wan, though that also could have just as easily been caused by a long winter of never getting outside. He had dark circles under his eyes, and she suspected he wasn't sleeping well, but pushing himself to get the work done as soon as possible could have contributed to that.

As Ava thought on it now, she couldn't put her finger on any one thing that made her feel like he was different this time around, it was simply more of an intuitive sense than anything. Sometimes in the evenings, as he spoke about the progress he'd made that day, as he joked and played with the kids, he looked happy, his words were filled with hope and joy, and yet...and yet his eyes seemed to be pleading to Ava somehow, as if trying to send her a secret message. If she asked what was wrong, he'd assure her nothing was, and then, almost as if to prove his vigor, later they'd gently make love.

Nonetheless, still, she felt like there was a need to be worried.

Sophie's giggles, louder this time, again made her smile, though this time she could clearly hear her daughter say, "Do you like it?" though, with her little kid pronunciation, it sounded more like *D'yu wike it?* She then mumbled something Ava again couldn't make out.

Ava put her book aside, rubbing her swollen belly. From where she sat gently rocking, she was able to see a good portion of the back yard beyond the fenced-in pool area. The end of term at the academy was always late May, after which time she planned to go on maternity leave. Ava wanted some time to prepare before her due date, and since she would have nearly a month to go yet, she wondered what she could do to keep herself busy. Perhaps putting in a small garden just beyond the pool would be a pleasant distraction, she thought. She'd never gardened before, but Ava felt like this was a wonderful chance to experiment with that.

If I can grow children in my belly, then surely cucumbers in the dirt are no problem.

Sophie, as if hearing her mother's internal joke, giggled again contentedly. *That's an odd echo*, Ava thought, as it almost sounded as if there were two laughs coming from the room next door.

Ava continued to rock gently as she rubbed her swollen belly, but now put her head back and closed her eyes to rest. One thing she had forgotten about being pregnant was how tiring it was, how much of her energy the baby pirated. She'd been doing a terrible job at rationing her energy, and she'd been coming home utterly exhausted, leaving dinner and childcare largely to Adam. As these next three months progressed, she told herself she'd have to be more aware of the fact she was nearly 50 years old, so taking things more slowly would be very wise. As she did, a strange coppery odor now came to her attention.

The afternoon sun slanted into her office, making it feel warm and cozy, and Ava felt sleep stealing upon her. As her rocking slowed and her body relaxed, the sound of Sophie laughing loudly interrupted that process for just a moment, but she felt the drift down continuing as she heard Sophie say, "Oh, Lizzie...*Ow, Wizzie.*

And then, with perfect clarity, she heard an echoed whisper respond, saying, *"Yes, Sophie?"*

Ava's head shot forward and her eyes popped open as she sucked in her breath, her heart immediately racing. She sat stock-still for a moment, not moving a muscle, confused whether she heard the voice in that weird wake-sleep borderline state of mind, or if there was actually someone in the room playing with her daughter. The minutes of silence as Ava listened carefully stretched on for what felt like an eternity, so much so she was acutely able to hear the ticking of the small clock she had on her desk. But all she heard was Sophie babbling to herself.

She was just about to relax again when, with perfect clarity, Ava heard the voice say, *"I love it, Sophie. It's perfect."*

Leaping out of her rocking chair with an anguished scream, Ava ran the few steps it took her to get to the door of the adjacent room. Though it literally took mere seconds to cover that short distance, Ava's mind raced in that time with thoughts of her daughter being harmed or killed or removed from the house before she would be able to get to her. Ava didn't think she would be able to manage the lifelong guilt she'd feel if anything happened to any of her children before she could intervene.

Calling out her daughter's name in one long howl, Ava burst through the cracked-open door, to find Sophie in the room totally alone. Sophie was coloring, surrounded by many pages of scribbled drawings, her dirty blond hair in pigtails, wearing the cute little sweatshirt with the goofy teddy bear face she loved so much. She looked up at her mother, her blue eyes the same color as her father's, chubby-cheeked ruddy face showing confused interest but no fear. The odor of copper hung so heavily in the room it was as if Ava could taste it.

"Yeah, Mommy?"

Ava stood at the door, looking around, shocked and confused. She scanned the room, finding it totally empty, seeing that none of the windows were open. It was totally empty save for what belonged in there. The only door to this room was the one she was now standing in, and so she would have seen someone trying to leave. This room was largely unfurnished, so there was simply nowhere for an intruder to hide.

Ava had to confront the obvious, that there was no one other than Sophie in this room, yet she had absolutely heard another voice in here only seconds ago.

"Sophie," she asked her daughter, who had gone back to coloring, "who were you talking to?"

"Lizzie," she said, distracted by her colored creation.

Ava reflexively scanned the room again, half expecting to see someone she'd somehow missed on the several other times she looked at the room. "Honey...who is Lizzie?"

"Her," Sophie said, pointing one plump finger to an empty corner near the fireplace.

Ava's mind raced for an explanation, yet she couldn't find one. She stood at the door, looking at Sophie coloring, to scanning the room, to Sophie, to the room, extremely confused. Then, she looked beyond Sophie for a moment and saw for the first time what she'd been drawing.

She picked up the several pieces of paper to view them better, and to her shock and horror, she realized Sophie was making drawings of horrific deaths. On one page she had scribble-drawn a picture of some people lighting others tied to a pole on fire, fat tears being shed by those burning alive. On another she saw a girl with bloody hair and an ax stuck in her head, and another with a black skeleton in flames, yet walking and scaring others. On the final colored page, she saw a drawing of a young, thin man in a formal suit, leering lecherously.

Yet despite all these drawings, ones Ava knew full well were typically only ever made by children who had witnessed dreadful traumas, the next picture she looked at was the one that filled her heart with terror and dismay. It was a simple pencil drawing of the strange, twisted symbol she'd seen all over Cromwell's Ferry on their visit that day, a drawing with lines that were too neat, straight, and precise to have been made by her four-year-old daughter. Ava glanced at the floor, seeing now one bright yellow pencil laying there, as a cold chill of fear crept up her spine.

She knew Sophie never drew with a pencil. She still found them too small for her inexperienced hand. Then, as an offhand addition to Sophie's explanation who Lizzie was, she said, "Her daddy hurts her."

A fear like none she had ever felt before abruptly seized her heart, so much so that Ava found it hard to draw breath for a moment, as she suddenly thought of some of the things the kids had said since they'd moved in. She recalled on their very first night here Sophie had said she liked Lizzie and Mel. Both she and Adam had assumed she'd meant kids at the preschool, but...did she? She remembered on Halloween night that Junior said he thought there were mice in the attic because of the scratching he could hear at night, and again Sophie had said there were scary things in Mel's attic. Junior had come into their room one night complaining about the monster in his closet, the one with glowing green eyes, but she'd taken him back to his room to show there was nothing in his closet but his clothes. Despite that, the next morning he'd said there was something in there staring at him all night, and that it stunk like something burned.

While all of these could be put aside as simply childish fears in an imposing new house (which is exactly what Ava had done, my Dear Friend), Ava now also had to confront the things she too had seen and heard over the months, things her rational mind had quickly dispensed with. She would see in her peripheral vision on many occasions what appeared to be shadows moving, yet every time she turned to look there was nothing there. On other occasions, Ava would think she caught the glimpse of fully formed people – people in colonial clothing, one in a Victorian-era suit, a Civil War-era soldier – but again, like the shadow people, as soon as she turned to view them fully there'd be nothing there.

These Ava had been able to dispense with as nothing but weird lighting, or the vagaries of how the brain interprets what the eye sees, but there was another event that she now had to confront, one she'd dispensed only through an act of will because she didn't want to think about it. One day during the long winter, as she passed by the open cellar door, Ava thought she heard the sound of a little girl down there weeping. Thinking Sophie was in the basement, hurt and all alone in the dark, Ava called out her name and went down to find her. She turned on the lights, and though they came on, they flickered annoyingly, as if there were a bad connection somewhere.

Standing at the bottom of the steps, Ava called out Sophie's name again loudly, trying to find her daughter. When at first she went down, the crying seemed to be coming from somewhere down the hall. Ava went from room to room trying to find Sophie, calling her name, opening every door to find the room empty, disoriented by the wildly flickering lights. When finally Ava reached the far room, the one with the weird stone table Adam loved but she hated, she felt that same chill of fear crawl up her spine as she realized she could now hear the unabated weeping coming from the colonial kitchen behind her, at the other end of the hall. As she quickly made her way back the hall, confused, trying to make sense of this and still hearing the soft weeping, she heard Sophie from the atop of the cellar steps, calling for her.

"Mommy?" she'd said from the top of the stairs, clutching a doll.

"Honey, are you alright?" Ava called as she swiftly trotted up the steps and the lights now finally came on fully. She tried hard to ignore that she could still hear weeping behind her. "I thought you were crying."

"Uh-nuh" Sophie said, shaking her head emphatically.

Scared, confused, her mind racing with unwanted possibilities, Ava closed the cellar door, shutting off the sound of the weeping below. She'd tried to forget about this event and had largely succeeded until now. Ava was a natural skeptic and always had been, but she was also a researcher. She believed in relying fully on the evidence one has, but when new data present themselves, the intellectually honest researcher must revise their hypothesis.

She was now being presented with unmistakably new data.

"Honey," Ava said, gently lifting Sophie to her feet as she took her hand, "Mommy was almost falling asleep in my office. Can you come play in there instead, and help Mommy stay awake?"

"OK, Mommy," she said pleasantly, trying to gather up the crayons on the floor.

"Never mind them, honey, just leave them. Mommy has markers in my office you can use."

Ava, working hard to maintain her composure, led Sophie

quickly to her office, but just before closing the door, she had the sudden idea to take some pictures of the empty room. She used her iPhone to take one overlapping picture after another, starting on her left and working her way to the right, until she'd snapped pics of the whole room. She then closed the door over gently behind her, though it remained open yet a crack.

Walking into her office, Ava got Sophie settled on the floor with some blank pieces of paper and markers from her desk, noting how much less coppery it smelled there. Once Sophie was cheerfully coloring again, Ava sat back down in her rocking chair to look at the pictures.

Ava had called up a pic on her phone, using her fingers to expand it, looking for anything out of the ordinary. She looked at the first and found nothing, then swiped it away. She opened the second and followed the same pattern, again seeing nothing but an empty room. Ava opened one pic after another, finding nothing but photos of an empty room each time.

Feeling silly and even a little foolish for thinking there might be something supernatural going on, Ava felt a bit of relief as she opened the last picture on her phone, spreading her fingers to expand the pic. Slowly scrolling over to the right, her heart almost stopped when, standing in the corner of the otherwise empty room, she now saw clearly the translucent image of a teenage girl with long brown hair. The girl wore an old-fashioned style nightie, and she would have looked otherwise normal if not for the fact she was transparent, looking like sickly pale green smoke glowing softly with some internal luminescence.

Ava, utterly shocked, put her hand to her mouth even as her eyes widened in disbelief. Her heart pounded, her breathing became difficult, and she felt almost dizzy with fear. She couldn't let herself scream because she didn't want to terrify Sophie, though at that moment terror is precisely what she felt. As Ava sat there, staring at this unbelievable image on her phone, she became aware that the coppery odor was now suddenly almost overpowering.

"Hi, Lizzie," Sophie said pleasantly, looking up at the door.

Ava, too afraid to move, too terrorized to look, yet feeling compelled to, slowly turned her head to look at the door as well. To her utter horror, she now saw the same young girl, a softly glowing translucent green, peering at her from around the partly open door. Though much of the girl's face was concealed by the door, Ava could see enough of her to know she was smiling at her even as she stared at Ava with her dead, pale corpse eyes. The girl held Ava in her gaze for a long moment, then slowly withdrew her still smiling face behind the door and closed it with a loud slam.

Choking on the scream she wanted to let out but swallowing it instead, Ava now swiftly gathered up Sophie and took her to the kitchen with her to begin dinner. As much as Ava would want to deny it, as much as her skeptical, non-believer mind wanted to reject it, there was no disputing one very clear, harshly cold fact: Her house was haunted.

She didn't know what to do, but she needed answers. Luckily, Ava knew exactly to whom to speak in order to get them.

[14]

"YOU KNOW, FOR ALL THE YEARS WE'VE KNOWN EACH other, I don't think I've ever been in your office before, Patrick," Ava said as she sat in Donegal's small Boston College office. Though still early April, this was the first truly warm day of the nascent spring, so Donegal had the one window in his office wide open, allowing in as much of the fresh spring air as possible. As the birds sang cheerily and sun shone brightly outside, and as Ava smelled the verdant odors on the warm breeze as she sat there, she thought it inconceivable that she was visiting her old friend to discuss living in a haunted house.

"Hmmm...," Donegal mused. "Yeah, I guess you're right. Well," he said, spreading his arms to offer her his very humble workspace, "what do you think?"

Ava looked around. She saw that while the furniture she'd had in her college office was modern, with slick lines and lots of glass and steel, the furniture in Donegal's office furnishings were decidedly traditional. She smiled to herself as she thought how perfectly that suited the priest. Donegal's office was classic and obdurate, much as was he.

She noted there were the ubiquitous pictures of the pope, of saints, and a Marian statue on the bookshelves, shelves that largely had theological titles on them, though she saw there were quite a variety of different books there. That didn't surprise her either, knowing how vast and wide was Donegal's intellect. She saw a book entitled *The Lesser Key of Solomon* on his desk, which she assumed to be a theological book, and another called *The History of Slattersburg*.

What did surprise her, though, were the paintings, photos, and prints of various unusual landscapes on the walls. Ava recognized one as being The Storr, while another was a painting of the Isle of Skye, both in Scotland. Another photo was of what appeared to be a random stone outcropping she didn't recognize, and then another was of an unknown castle, dark and foreboding. There were other prints equally unknown to her.

She looked at her still smiling friend and said, "I like it. It suits you perfectly."

Donegal chuckled as he said, "Well, it'd better. I spend enough of my time in here."

The pair shared a laugh at that, followed by a moment of heavy quiet as Ava sat in silence, wondering what exactly she was doing there. As the silence grew, Donegal said, "So...what brings you here today, Ava? You said you needed help with something, but only wanted to discuss it in person."

Ava continued to sit in silence as she turned that simple question over in her mind. *What do you want?* she asked herself, looking out the window to the largely empty courtyard beyond. She'd asked to come on Good Friday because her kids didn't have school, but she also knew classes weren't held during Holy Week at this Catholic college, either. Ava had wanted to avoid seeing any former colleagues if she could. Rather than feeling clever, however, she felt like she was sneaking back to talk to Donegal because she knew how ridiculous her fears were.

Finally finding her words, she looked at the priest and said simply, "It's complicated."

He sat back in his chair and silently gestured for her to go on. Ava then told him everything about the family's entire history with the house, from visiting Cromwell's Ferry to Adam's sudden infatuation with it, from his buying it without discussing it with her to the many accidents and one death that occurred during the renovations, from Junior saying he heard things in the attic to his saying there was something in his room, from her sense of being watched that first day to her perpetual sense of the air being stuffy, listless, and close. She told him the story of her weird experience in the basement all the way to her most recent encounter with the ghostly girl just a few weeks prior, showing him the picture on her phone.

The entire time Ava spoke, Donegal sat back in his leather desk chair, paying careful attention to what she said. He at first looked implacable, simply an impassive listener to her story. As more and more details of the story emerged, the more he seemed pained.

When Ava concluded, Donegal thought for some time, gently rubbing his chin in deep, wordless thought.

"Patrick?" Ava said at last.

He looked at her, stopping as if suddenly aware of her presence.

A vague fear and dread had slowly started gnawing at her as her story went on and his reaction changed with each additional detail. She'd hoped he would immediately put aside her fears as the workings of an overtired, hormone-clouded mind, but that didn't seem to be the case at all. "What's going on, Patrick? What do you think?"

Rather than immediately answering, he instead asked a question. "You say this girl, this ghost girl, drew something, am I correct? A random design. May I please see it?"

Ava rummaged around in her bag for a moment, trying to find the piece of paper she had folded in there, then handed it to Donegal. He unfolded it, looking at it intently as he again rubbed his temples as if stricken by a terrible headache.

Donegal looked at the picture for some time, then said, "Well, Ava, I can tell you your house isn't haunted..."

Ava could almost feel the tension inside her begin to melt away in an instant. *No, of course, it isn't. What even a foolish thing for me to* −

"It's demon-possessed," he said, completing his thought.

Ava stared at his kind face mutely, dumbly. She was shocked and confused, the words he'd just said echoing in her head as she tried to assign meaning to them but finding actual comprehension elusive. Ava felt it was like trying to grasp an object that was too well slicked, one that would maddeningly slip away as soon as she had hold of it. Because Donegal's novel use of these old words was so shockingly new to her, Ava simply sat there utterly baffled and dazed, feeling almost like she'd just been hit over the head.

"De...demon possessed? I don't...what is...Patrick, what does that even mean?" she asked at last, her emotions finally getting the better of her as frustrated tears welled in her eyes.

"Ava, listen to me very carefully, because this is incredibly important," Donegal said earnestly. "I know full well you don't share my beliefs, but at this point what you believe or don't believe in is no longer relevant. You're going to have to accept that certain things you've never thought possible, things you probably thought were ridiculous fantasies, are real. Very, *very* real, and some of these things are in your house right now."

She stared at him, wiping her eyes, still trying to make sense of what he was saying. "OK, fine," she finally said. "Tell me what's going on."

Donegal thought for a moment, gathering his words, steepled fingers at his chin, looking almost as if in prayer. "You said you feared your house was haunted because you saw a ghost and you heard whispers. That would certainly sound like the case if not for some of the other things you explained. From what I've studied, that feeling you have, the stuffiness and still air, that's the malevolence of demon. Its evil, its perverted spirit being so intense that we can actually *feel* it, but since we can't really register what's happening, we interpret it as warm, humid air. If your house were just haunted then it'd be chilly, with cold pockets whenever there's a ghost."

Ava's eyes darted around the office, trying to grasp what he was saying. *A demon? This can't be real! This can't possibly be real!* She looked back outside, seeing a few happy young people walking out there, their faces turned towards the midday sun, reveling in the feel of a soft warm breeze on their skin. *That's real. People and the sun and the wind. Demons can't be real. They just can't be...can they?!*

She attended to Donegal again, feeling literally stunned by this information as he went on.

"That symbol, that shape the girl drew," he said, pointing at the pencil drawing. "It's not random. It's the sigil of a demon named Andromelech. He's – well, I say 'he,' but of course demons have no gender, regardless of how they appear – he's very powerful, very twisted and perverse, and exceedingly evil."

This new information was almost too much for Ava to manage. *So not only are there demons but now they have names?!* Everything she thought was nothing but a foolish notion, the entire way she understood the world and approached creation, an entire paradigm built up over almost half a century, crumbled down to pieces in moments. It was simply too much, so in this moment of primal confusion, Ava's mind chose to focus on something simpler and more direct. "What's a sigil?"

"Oh, umm..." Donegal said, taken aback a little by Ava focusing on that one small detail. "It's like a symbol or a sign that represents a demon. It's almost like its true, secret name. Sorcerers use it when summoning a demon, or worshippers will use it when offering sacrifices to a demon to honor it."

Ava's mind now swam with all this new information, matters that earlier today she would have dispensed as unlikely, ones that a year ago she would have disparaged as foolish. *And yet, here I now am, talking to a priest on Good Friday about demons' sigils, magic users, and devil worshippers. Lovely.* Ava was so overwhelmed with this new, incomprehensible information that she almost felt lightheaded.

"Now, Ava, this is very important," Donegal went on. "Andromelech is one of the most vicious and twisted demons in the entire hellish hierarchy. He is horribly perverse and takes great delight in twisting things that are good into aberrant, evil versions of themselves. One thing that has always been associated with him is violence, but most especially sexual violence. There is almost nothing that pleases him more than taking that beautiful expression of love between two married people and turning it into a sick, evil act of power, torment, and pain. His worshippers have always used violent rape as a way of honoring this foul beast. It's like he feeds off the pain, the violence, and the horror of it."

Once again, the overarching information proved too daunting, simply too much for Ava to focus on in that moment, despite her incredibly sharp and agile mind. So, she focused on something smaller and more manageable. "You said, 'always been associated with him.' You mean there's a history of these things?"

"Oh, yes," Donegal said. "Demons and demonic activity have been documented for as long as people have been writing anything at all. If you were to go back and read the ancient writings you will see demons everywhere in the world, all over the world. I suspect their presence with us goes back far earlier than that. They've always been with us, forever trying to twist us to do evil, to do each other harm. To become as evil as they."

"They want to kill us?" Ava asked, still feeling dazed.

"Oh, no, not at all. What's death to a demon? A person is either lost in sin, so the demons already have them, or saved, in which case the demons can't reach them. No, what they want is to turn us towards evil, to torment us for their own evil pleasure, make us do terrible acts of evil, for us to harm others, kill others, kill ourselves. They utterly delight in all that evil."

She looked at her old friend, one who clearly had facets of which she was not at all aware. "How do you know all this, Patrick? I mean, this isn't part of what you get taught at seminary, is it?"

"No, not at all. I studied all this on my own after I developed an interest in demonology. You know I've worked with poor people all over the world. I came to realize that there were forces that tortured people, forces much larger than even corrupt governments and greedy, powerful elites." He stopped, thinking for a moment, then added, "When you look carefully enough, you realize there are powers at work against us much larger than we are. I've seen the evil influence of demons not just on people and families, but even entire cities and whole countries. It's really sickening, the more you know."

Ava now rubbed her own temples, as Donegal had earlier. "This is all just too much...too much. So, does this Andrama...Adremel..."

"Andromelech."

"OK, sure. He has a history you're familiar with?"

"Yes, sadly. He has a very long and wicked history. Andromelech was actually worshipped in Sumer as a god. He..." Donegal looked away, obviously now trying to find the right words and having trouble doing so.

"He what?" Ava said after a moment. "What, Patrick? He what?"

Donegal sighed, clearly uncomfortable and not wanting to say what came next. "This is going to be difficult for you to hear, Ava, especially under the circumstances, but you must hear it. Of all the good and pure things Andromelech revels in perverting, nothing gives him greater pleasure than harming children. In Sumer, when he was worshipped there as a god, people would sacrifice their babies to him by throwing them, living and screaming, into the flames of his temple."

Ava sucked in her breath with that last statement, one hand covering her mouth while the other, instinctively and protectively, went to her swollen belly. She felt nauseous and even more light-headed.

"Patrick, you can't...are my children safe?"

"In a word, Ava, no. No, they are not. Not as long as they live in that house."

This was too much for Ava. She'd come to speak to Donegal because she feared her house was haunted, but she hoped and truly expected him to tell her things were simply not what she thought they were. At the very worst, she thought he'd say houses are haunted sometimes, but, *c'est la vie, non?* What she absolutely didn't expect Donegal to say was that demons, things she thought were nothing but fantasy game tropes and fodder for old legends, were not only real, but that there was actually one living in her house – oh, and not only was there a demon in her house, but it was a child-hating, sexually perverse fallen Sumerian god. This was far beyond too much for Ava. She could take it no more.

"No," she said now, standing as she emphatically shook her head. "No, no, no, uh-uh, no, no way, nada, NO!" she finally yelled. "This *isn't* happening. This *can't* be happening. I don't believe *any* of this and, quite frankly, I think all this is *bullshit!*"

"Ava," Donegal said, speaking softly. "I know this must be incredibly hard for you, and I understand your shock, but like I said, what you believe now doesn't matter anymore."

"*NO!*" she yelled again, glad there were so few students outside. "No, this can't be...this just can't be happening to us. This is too much, this can't be real..." she said, now slumping back down into her chair, hand on her aching head.

"Ava, please get your phone and bring up the picture you took of the girl." She did as Donegal asked, and when she had it, he motioned for the phone. He expanded it so the girl's ghostly translucent, greenish face took up the entire screen, then showed it to Ava. "Is this real? Did this really happen? You convinced yourself you never heard the crying in your basement, even though you know full well you did. *This* you cannot deny. This is as real as it gets. And if she's in your house, you can bet there are others as well, but not all the spirits there are going to be so playful and kind as her."

Ava stared at Donegal, feeling defeated.

"You came here asking for help. This is the best help I can offer, Ava." He handed the phone back to her, saying, "I know you don't want this to be. I don't want it to be, but it is. We need to fight against this evil."

Ava thought back to the night she and Adam had the fight about buying the house, and then her conversation with Donegal as they stood admiring the statue of Saint Michael defeating Lucifer. She recalled thinking then about the overwhelming nature of evil, wondering if there was anything we could really do against it, wondering even if there were times when the evil of the world was simply too much for us, too strong, too powerful.

Ava now thought of the danger her children were in, and, as she did, she felt clear-minded and centered for the first time since they'd started this bizarre conversation. As her thoughts focused and her mind cleared even more, she balled up her hands into two fists of fierce determination. She thought, *Let's fuck this demon up.*

"OK, fine. So, what do we do? Have an exorcism? Can you do that?"

Donegal smiled broadly at her fighting pluck. "Now, there's the Ava I know. No, I can't do exorcisms. I'm just an enthusiastic amateur, neither trained nor authorized by the Vatican to do them. But I can reach out to the archdiocese to consult with the exorcist there about this issue for you. I know him personally, Father Miguel Villalobos. A fine young man, whom I'm sure will be able to help."

As Ava left and started her two-hour drive back home, she felt a strange sense of comfort, something she realized she'd not felt in a long time. She took a deep breath, held it for a moment, and then let it out slowly, focusing and relaxing herself. One thing she knew, after speaking to Donegal, was that living in that house until they were able to plan for the exorcism was going to be challenging. She believed sending the kids to Adam's parents in California until this was all settled might make the most sense.

Ava also knew she'd have to come up with an excuse why she wanted to send them away, because something told her not mentioning her meeting with Donegal and her plans for the exorcism to Adam would be best. She didn't know what it was, and she didn't know why, but she completely agreed that was for the best.

[15]

At the exact same time Ava sat in Donegal's office having her world view torn apart, Adam sat slouched in his desk chair as the voices and the images conspired against him to shred his sanity. He stared blankly at nothing, moaning and crying out occasionally as he did, as if trapped in a nightmare. Junior was in his room and Sophie was taking a nap, so he felt no pretense to make it appear he was writing his book.

"Take what you want, Adam. Take everything you want."

The voices had become increasingly clear, and though there was always an underlying, roiling cacophony of whispering, a sentence or two would constantly come to the surface that Adam could easily make out. It was like churning waters that would dredge up things from a riverbed, only to have them float down again into the watery darkness. In addition to words being whispered, Adam could now also hear an entire other chorus of screams, people crying out in pain and horror, of people begging for mercy, people dying in agony.

"Noooooo..." Adam muttered to himself weakly, trying to

fight off an evil over which he had no control. "Noooooooooo...I will not..."

"If it feels good, do it."

In the past few weeks, the voices had become more demanding in their insistence that Adam commit terrible acts of violence against his family. While they at first were altogether too quiet to make out when he'd started to hear the whispers, and then they had turned into evil taunting and mocking, the whispering had recently become nothing but a constant, unending assault on his reason, a relentless campaign to make him hurt his family members, especially through sexual violence.

In this, the voices were joined by the images he was now being forced to view.

"It's all yours...take it."

Adam had already been compelled to repeatedly watch the entire history of violent sexual acts that had occurred on this site over the years, but now he was included in these images, and rather than watching as if only a spectator, he saw them through his own eyes, a fully involved participant.

He was a tribal warrior raping a captured woman, then slitting her throat at the wolf mage's feet; *he* was Uzziah attacking a slave in a cellar storage room as he punched her as hard as he thrust into her; *he* was Rosa Kreuz, holding down a little boy by the neck that she had bent face down over a table, slowly inserting an oversized piece of wood inside him; *he* was Samuel King ravaging his own daughter; *he* was Mortimer St. Germain anally raping Carmella, delighting in twisting her raven black hair into his fist and pushing her face into a pillow even as her blood began to flow. Adam was all these beasts, each of these sexual monsters, and so many more.

And whereas he had once been repulsed by these images, whereas he'd once hated his arousal, though he was loathe to admit it, the sense of power and control delighted him wickedly. The voices tempted him incessantly and encouraged him to feel pleasure in this violence, and that if something pleased him, he could simply take it by force if he wanted... even from his own family, even from his children.

He took out his painfully hard cock, stroking it against his will.

"You know you want to. If you want it, just take it."

"Nooooo...nooo...stop, please stop..." Adam moaned, growing weaker, losing this fight, and with it, his sanity. While he might now delight savagely in the power he felt from the past sexual violence, he couldn't stand seeing his family involved. Yet the images didn't seem to care: In addition to showing the historical acts of sexual horror committed there, Adam was now also being shown glimpses of a possible future, a future in which he becomes as much of an evil beast as any of the others who lived in this house and abused their children.

"I won't...I won't..." he groaned, weaker and weaker.

"Everything is yours...all you have to do is take it."

"I can't...I won't...I...I...I caaaaaaaaa..." he trailed off in a harsh, choked whisper, as his will finally broke, and he gave himself fully over to the will of the demon.

Adam stood suddenly, putting himself back into his pants. He walked resolutely upstairs to where his children lay, a hard look of cold purpose on his face. He opened Sophie's door, and there he found his little girl sleeping happily, a bit of drool smeared on her ruddy cheeks. Adam stood there a moment, watching her as she slept. Then he gently closed her door all the way.

He walked the few paces to Junior's room, where he found the door wide open. Adam stood in the doorway, staring blankly at his son. To the small sliver of Adam that remained actively involved in his own mind, his dull stare felt like one of his mindless sleepwalks. There he stood, silently, until Junior noticed his father. Junior was watching something on his iPad and wasn't aware of Adam's presence for some time. He then looked over at him suddenly, surprised to see Adam simply standing there.

"Dad?" he asked, unnerved.

Still Adam merely stood there, staring deeply at his son. He didn't say a word, didn't blink, hardly appeared to breathe. Instead, he just stared.

Feeling a fear, dark and unreasonable, gathering within him, Junior pushed himself back into the headboard of his bed to get away from this baleful image that was his own father. He would have pushed himself through the wall and sprouted wings if that would have gotten him away from Adam's awful stare.

"*Daaaaaaaaaad?*" he said, almost whining, pleading for some kind of release from that implacable stare.

And yet, stare for a few moments more is all Adam did. Then, all at once, he licked his lip like a snake tasting the air, and rushed in at his son, pouncing, grabbing him by the neck. Adam lifted his son off his bed and began to drag him upstairs to the attic.

"Daddy?" Junior whispered weakly until the fear, shock, and amazement of what was happening took his voice.

[16]

IN THE FRONT ATTIC ROOM, BENT OVER A PLAIN WOODEN
chair, looking with unfocused eyes at the window in that
room, Junior's shocked 7-year-old's mind could not fully
register or understand what was being done to him, or why.
The pain in his body was mirrored perfectly by the hurt he
felt in his heart.

Looking at the window, disconnected from what was
happening, from what his father was doing to him, Junior
closed his eyes hard. When he reopened them, he was
amazed to see there was another person in the room with
them. A young man, bearded, pale, and thin, wearing a black
suit, shirt, and tie, stood there now, watching with a smirk,
gloved hands clasped before him. Junior looked at the man,
thinking for a moment help of some strange kind had arrived.

He reached out to the man, whispering "Help...me..."
before Adam grabbed his arm, holding it down once again.

The man watched intently, seeming to enjoy the spectacle
rather than having any intention of helping. As Junior looked
at him, hoping yet for rescue, he watched as the man smiled
broadly, widely, far too wide for any human mouth to stretch,

as impossibly long, sharp teeth pushed aside his smiling lips. Watching still, horrified yet strangely unable to look away or even close his eyes, Junior saw as the man, unclasping his hands and stretching out his arms, was swiftly wreathed in a burst of green, violet, and indigo ethereal flames. The flames fanned out arcing behind him, danced around him, yet consumed neither the man nor his surroundings.

Junior, unable to shut his wide-open eyes, screamed, and continued to scream until his throat was raw, until his father clasped his hand around his mouth. Still he screamed, the sound muffled by Adam's palm until finally his howls slowly trailed off as his throat gave way.

He screamed because he'd watched as the man had suddenly transformed into some mind-crushingly horrible beast. This beast stood as tall as the arched roof of the attic, yet wreathed still in the dancing flames, with the head of a horned black wolf, rows of long teeth protruding out of his leering mouth. This beast had the upper body of a human, but of an inhumanly dark, blood-red color, with long black claws rather than fingertips, and the shaggy legs of a wolf as well. Huge, black, raven-like wings protruded out of its back, fully opened as if about to take flight.

The beast's yellow snake eyes looked deeply into Junior's, and as they did, the boy began to laugh insanely.

It stood there, yellow eyes boring into Junior's, until at once it roared loudly, making an unearthly sound that no wild beast has ever made, or is even capable of making. It roared at Junior with all its power and all its might, hatred, and anger, roaring so loudly Junior could feel it inside him. It roared so long and so forcefully that Junior felt like he was adrift in the roar, falling through it for years, for eons, maybe forever...

[17]

AVA DROVE HOME FROM BOSTON THAT DAY AS FAST AS SHE safely could, the lovely early spring landscape racing by unnoticed. Her mind was entirely too preoccupied with the conversation she'd had with Donegal for her to appreciate the warm sun or brightly budding trees. She especially kept turning over his words when she'd pointedly asked him if her children were safe in their home.

No, they are not. Those words echoed in her head like a ticking clock keeping track of how long it was taking her to get home and how far she was from securing her children's safety.

When Ava made the final turn from the corkscrew around the hill to the straightaway leading to her house, she looked on it now with vastly different eyes. What might normally appear to be a nothing but a gorgeously restored colonial mansion on a bright sunny day suddenly seemed to her a dreadful monument, looming, and full of evil. Living there had always been a compromise on her part due to Adam's overwhelming enthusiasm for the house, but Ava now looked at her home with loathing as she drove up to it.

Ava entered the quiet house, and immediately had a sense of dread because of the crypt-like silence in it. She could normally hear some kind of bustling activity as soon as she walked in the house, whether it was Sophie's never-ending prattling and singing, or Junior's current favorite show on the iPad, or even the sound of Adam's typing and his favorite music coming from the study.

But this was a silence like death.

"Hello?" Ava said nervously, as she tried to keep down her anxiety. As she took a few tentative steps into the foyer, her heart pounding, still she received no answer and could hear nothing but the echoes of her footfalls on the cold marble floor. Her mind raced with all the worst things that could be happening to explain this sudden silence, possibilities made even more horrible by her recent conversation with Donegal. Despite her best efforts, her increasing anxiety was swiftly turning into gnawing fear.

"*HELLO?!*" she said more loudly, her voice beginning to shake with a nervousness bordering on panic.

Then, as she took a few more hesitant steps into the foyer, she saw through the rear French doors a flash as Adam raced by, laughing loudly, Sophie gleefully chasing him with a stick. Rushing to the doors, Ava stood there a moment, almost shocked by this perfectly normal and happy domestic scene, and then, realizing she'd been holding her breath, let it out in a long sigh. A sense of relief like none she'd ever felt before poured over Ava, and she could feel the stress melting out of her tense muscles.

Ava leaned her head against the glass as she watched her husband and daughter play. This was one of Sophie's favorite games, the one where she was a knight of old slaying the beastly dragon, a role Adam played with energy and aplomb, holding fingers to his head to make the horns and doing his best dragon roar. He'd run and run, Sophie chasing him with

ANTONIO RICARDO SCOZZE

her stick until finally, the dragon would give in to his wounds, falling to the ground with a great, pathetic cry. But, proving that even wounded dragons are dangerous, Adam would always grab Sophie and tickle her until she shrieked in delight.

Ava stood there watching this, the love and tenderness she was seeing in her family just too much to bear, when, scanning the back yard for Junior, she suddenly realized he was nowhere to be seen.

Junior would normally be somewhere nearby kicking around his soccer ball, and though slaying the dragon was Sophie's game, he would typically take advantage of the situation to join in on the fun and pounce his father as well. Sometimes that would annoy Adam, but nonetheless Junior could still be counted on doing it every time they played this game.

Until now.

Ava scanned the backyard more carefully, again feeling that sense of fear and loathing creep down her spine, like a spider crawling along her back. She looked intently at the fenced-in area where the kids were allowed to play, hoping that she had somehow simply missed seeing her son earlier. Though their total acreage on the hilltop was vast, the area within the fence where they let the kids play wasn't overly large, and there really was nowhere for Junior to hide from her view at the back doors.

Ava turned away, wondering where Junior might be, beginning to feel overwhelmingly uneasy. She called his name but received nothing back save for icy quiet from the house just as she had before. Thinking that perhaps he was upstairs for some reason, Ava walked up towards the second floor, calling out his name every few steps. The ongoing, stony silence made a sense of impending disaster settle queasily in her belly, and she took each step up with an inescapable sense of something horrible awaiting her.

At the top of the stairs Ava again called Junior's name, and again was met with nothing but stillness. As she took a few steps towards his room, thinking perhaps he was simply watching a show on the tablet with earbuds in, Ava realized she could hear his voice, softly singing, coming from the attic, the door to which had been left wide open.

She had another great sense of relief and melting of tension, but this was quickly halted when she thought *Why is he in the attic all alone?*

Ava slowly walked up the creaking steps, hearing his soft singing more clearly. Once at the top, she wasn't quite certain from which room it was coming. The attic was set up much like the cellar far below, with the steps leading to a central hall, larger room on either end and several smaller ones arrayed along the hallway. All these rooms had in the past been servants' quarters.

She looked down the hall to the front room, where she saw bright sunlight pouring in through the open door. It sounded like that's where the singing was coming from. Ava walked in that direction, fear fighting to utterly take over her mind, though she struggled hard against it, pushing it down in an act of overt will.

"Junior?" Ava called once but received no answer. As she approached the room, she finally was able to see her son, sitting on a wooden chair with his back towards the door, staring out the window, alone in this otherwise unfurnished room. She relaxed a little, but only slightly due to the bizarre nature of this entire situation.

"Junior, what are you..." Ava had started to say but abruptly stopped when, upon taking several more steps towards the doorway, she all at once realized how many things were horribly wrong. Junior merely sat there singing, not responding to his mother at all, with his head leaning over awkwardly to the side, as if suddenly too heavy for his neck to keep it upright. His left arm hung limply at his side, his right hand lay dead in his lap. He wore nothing but a tee-shirt, and the odor of urine hung vaguely in the air. As Ava slowly stepped closer and closer, she could see her son's brown hair had suddenly turned pale, as if doused in bleach.

"Junior..." she whispered harshly, the fear now utterly taking her heart.

"I saw three ships come sailing in, sailing in, sailing in..." Ava heard him singing softly, the same refrain he'd been repeating the whole time, "I saw three ships come sailing in, at three o'clock in the morning..."

"Junior?" she said weakly one final time, almost as if pleading for this to be some kind of horrible prank.

Ava slowly walked to her son, dreading what she was about to see. She sucked in her breath and her eyes widened in horrid surprise when she, at last, saw the terror awaiting her. As her son continued to inanely sing to himself, Ava could see his hazel eyes were bulging out of their sockets, his sclera turned a dry, angry red from not blinking. His whitened hair stood up crazily all around his head, his mouth twisted and turned into a perpetual, mad smile, his lips stretched so thin they had cracked in several places. Drool poured out of the corners of his mouth and clung to his chin.

Still he sang endlessly, "I saw three ships come sailing in, sailing in, sailing in...I saw three ships come sailing in, at three o'clock in the morning..."

Ava, crying, rushed in and fell to her knees to take her son, her first-born child into her arms, holding him close to her and gently rocked him. As she lifted him up, she saw that he was sitting in a puddle of his urine. Shocked, disgusted, terrified, and confused, the only thing Ava knew to do in that moment was to clutch her beloved little child to her and rock, pressing his small body to hers as if somehow her touch alone could heal him of this horror. Junior didn't respond at all his mother's touch, remaining as limp and lifeless as a rag doll, his wild-eyed and toothy smile remaining unchanged. The only sign of life was his soft, ceaseless singing.

"I saw three ships come sailing in, sailing in, sailing in...I saw three ships come sailing in, at three o'clock in the morning..."

Ava's tears flowed freely, as she began to suspect this horrible event, the terror living in her house with them, would prove too much for her psyche to manage, and that she would soon go mad. She cried for her son until she nearly gagged on her tears.

Ava cried and cried, as her son did nothing but sing quietly to himself. "I saw three ships come sailing in, sailing in, sailing in...I saw three ships come sailing in, at three o'clock in the morning..."

As Ava held on to her son, rocking gently, she heard the distant sound of howling, a gut-wrenching, heart-breaking sound of someone screaming in unfathomable grief, fear, and rage. Ava wondered for a moment who that could possibly be, and it was not until her own throat began to ache that she realized it was she who was screaming.

[18]

ELLIE SANDERS SAT AT HER DESK AT THE REGIONAL Department of Children and Families office, carefully inspecting her red painted nails as she listened with growing annoyance to an angry mother who pleaded for the return of her children.

"Ellie, I just don't understand," the woman said, her voice tremulous as she tried to maintain her composure.

"What is there to understand, Rachel?" Ellie answered dismissively, as she pushed her cat-eyes glasses back up her petite nose. "You endangered your children, you were reported, the state stepped in, and now they're being placed in foster care for their safety. What about that don't you understand?"

Come on, you dumb shit, Ellie thought. *Say something, I know you want to.*

"I'm a good mother..." Rachel answered, her quivering voice breaking as she began to sob loudly. "I've never hurt my kids...I would never hurt my kids...I could never...I've done nothing wrong, Ellie! Why did the state take my kids?! Why are you doing this to me?!"

"I'm not doing anything to you," Ellie answered sternly. "You did this to yourself. You did this to your children. You were the one who decided to leave an eleven-year-old girl alone watching her two younger sisters, a ten- and an eight-year-old. That was reckless and dangerous."

That should push a few buttons.

"I didn't have a choice!" Rachel snapped back at Ellie. "You know I'm working two jobs, barely making ends meet. I get nothing from Jay, you know that. They were alone in the apartment for, like, a half-hour before I got home. I've never done anything wrong, and the one time something happens I lose my children?!"

"That's the job of the government, Rachel," Ellie said, her high-pitched, almost girl-like voice attaining its best disinterested bureaucratic tone. "To protect children from abusive or neglectful parents like you."

Here it comes...

"Why, you fucking bitch!" Rachel now shrieked at Ellie through the phone. "You fucking cunt! You snotty little know-it-all piece of shit fucking bitch! You don't even have any kids, who are you to tell me shit?! How *dare* you call me neglectful?!"

"If the shoes fits, Rachel..."

"You...you..." Rachel said, choking on her words due to her rage. "You fucking piece of shit whore! You fucking scum! If I could reach through this phone, I'd fucking choke you, you cunt! I swear to God, you'd better be careful walking down the street because if I ever see you, I'm going to fucking run you over, you fucking bitch!"

Got you.

Ellie smiled coolly, wishing Rachel a good day. The calls to the DCF are regularly recorded, so now there was documentation of Rachel threatening Ellie, a government employee, engaged in the course of her official state duties.

As soon as she disconnected from Rachel, Ellie filed an official complaint with the police, knowing that she'd soon be visited by two serious-looking state police officers, thus beginning what was likely to be a long relationship with the legal system. The charges Rachel was about to have filed against her, as well as the additional complications legal issues would create with her work and finances, all but assured she wouldn't see her children again for a long time. By then, Ellie thought contentedly, Rachel most likely wouldn't even recognize them anymore.

Ellie sat back in her desk chair, her small mouth smiling smugly. She felt exceedingly pleased with the work she'd done on this case. As she reflected upon it, Ellie supposed it was just for a case like this that she'd been led to get into such work. When she'd graduated with her degree in social work, many of her classmates said they'd never work for DCF due to the soul-crushing duties, or at the very least only work there long enough to get some experience.

She'd been there several years by this point, and always felt it was nothing short of a privilege to make certain children wound up in the best environments for them, so they could get everything they needed in life. Having been through the system herself, Ellie knew full well the guidance, support, and treatment kids needed to not just survive but to thrive. She was proud she was able to take children from neglectful, uncaring, unhinged parents like Rachel and send them to the right families for upbringing.

Ellie was also very pleased by her work because, especially in cases like the one with Rachel and her children, she was able to feed the needs of her coven, and in so doing, further her fanatical devotion to Satan. She particularly delighted in taking children from poor families and sending them to the best environments, like the Konig family, where Rachel's daughters had been placed. The

Konigs were also part of Ellie's coven, and she knew those young girls were about to experience the very best treatment.

Ellie thought of the first coven house she was sent to as a little girl in the system as she looked at the tattoo on her left wrist of an orange-winged butterfly, one wing disconnected from the body. She'd often wondered if that wing was being put back in place, thereby making the butterfly whole again, or was it being torn off, perhaps as a punishment for failure? Ellie had never been able to pries out the mystery behind that.

It was at the coven house that Ellie felt like she'd finally found a true family, people she could count on, something in which she could believe. They were a family very much like the Konigs, firm but fair, loving yet dedicated to something much bigger than themselves. Ellie had received the training she'd been desperate for, the discipline she ached for in her life, and the direction she needed to not become a worthless heroin junkie like her mother. She looked back fondly on those years, especially the early days of training when she was just first beginning to grasp her purpose in life and the ways in which she might serve. It was something she knew Rachel's children would soon be experiencing, and she felt truly happy for them.

There were times of pain, certainly, but what life-affirming transformative process doesn't have pain? Ellie could still recall the placid faces of the men, the many older men in suits, that she danced for the first night she was deemed worthy of doing so. She'd wondered if she was pleasing them, she'd worried that perhaps she wasn't fulfilling her duty to the coven, but then later their bodies expressed an obvious appreciation their faces had not. Later that night, when her foster mother washed off her makeup and cleaned up the scratches and bruises, cooing to her how magnificently she had accomplished her job, Ellie recalled feeling a pride like nothing she'd ever felt before.

There were sacrifices, but what growth is there in life without sacrifice? Ellie distinctly recalled her first sacrifice, at age 13, when she'd been admitted into the coven as a full member. He was a younger foster brother of hers, and though Ellie had long since forgotten his name, she could clearly remember his curly blond hair and his eyes peering up at her from the altar just before she drew the blade of the dagger across his throat. Ellie had peered down at him coldly, never once hesitating as she made the slice deep into his neck, not for a moment did she even consider failing to make the sacrifice. Ellie was zealously dedicated to her coven, for which she was willing to do literally anything.

As she thought about the long road that had taken her to this point and reflected on how pleased she was with Rachel's case, Ellie checked her next appointment. She had a meeting in ten minutes with a woman named Ava Rosenburg-Long to discuss the strange case of her son's sudden mental breakdown and fugue state.

She'd been assigned this case two months earlier, when the 51-A report filed by the hospital reached the DCF. Though the report triggered the mandated investigation by DCF, it had intentionally been misdirected from the beginning by the emergency room doctor who'd first seen the boy. Having received orders from the coven, he'd documented the boy's shattered mental state and obvious physical issues but deliberately omitted any details that would suggest sexual abuse. Once so documented by a board-certified medical professional, it afterward became a fact nothing of an untoward nature had occurred while he was alone with his father.

Ellie could distinctly recall the day she'd been given the Long case. She'd been talking with another mother like

Rachel when she was asked to report to the unit director's office immediately. Mr. Nero was several steps above in the chain of command, so such a request was unexpected and exciting. Ellie knew he was also highly placed in the coven command structure, so she felt a special thrill when ordered to see him for the first time. She'd checked the bright red lipstick on her full lips, double-checked the tight bun of her dark hair, then smoothed her leopard-print skirt before reporting to her superior.

Finding the door to his office open, she'd knocked on the frame as she walked in. "You wanted to see me, sir?" Ellie asked.

Nero smiled as he looked up from his work and saw her. "Yes, I do. Thank you for coming so quickly, Ellie. I have here a special case I'd like you to work on," he said as he handed her a plain red file folder. "This is a case The Commission has asked that you, personally, handle."

Looking over the details of the case, Ellie had looked up from the file folder confused into Nero's fat, bespectacled face. "Commission, sir? What commission?"

"*The* Commission, Ellie," his soft voice almost trembling with excitement. "Our regional council of The Commission is requesting you manage this case."

Ellie gasped slightly, never once thinking she'd be so honored to be assigned a task by The Commission itself, or even by a regional council of it. The Luciferian sigil she'd had branded into her side after making her first sacrifice tingled with delighted anticipation at this honor.

Nero smiled lecherously at Ellie, his pasty white skin slick with sweat as he said, "I made a personal recommendation to the council, knowing the quality of your talents."

It was all these talents Ellie planned to use in the successful completion of this case; she would not fail her coven. First, she had to deal with the mother, Ava.

Ellie went to the conference room where she found Ava waiting. "It's good to see you again, Ava," she said, shaking her hand. "I wish it could be under better circumstances."

"Yes, thank you," Ava said. Ellie noted it looked like the dark rings under her eyes had grown since the last she'd seen her, and she clearly had recently wept. "This has been so hard on everyone."

"I'm sure it has been...but, oh, my," Ellie said, pointing at Ava's impressive belly. "That boy is going to be a big one. I think you've grown since last time. When are you due?"

"In just a few weeks. I'm definitely ready to meet this little guy, especially...after everything that's happened."

"Well, I appreciate you coming on your own as I requested, so we could discuss the findings and so we could go over some things I thought you might prefer to hear alone."

Ava shifted in her seat, looking uncomfortable. *I do love that look, that squirm*, Ellie thought.

"First of all, I want to reassure you that the Hopewell Institute is one of the finest treatment centers we could possibly hope to find for a case like Adam's..."

"Junior," Ava interrupted. "We always call him Junior."

Ellie smiled patiently. "Of course. In a case like Junior's. Hopewell has been specializing in the treatment of children since after World War One, so they have a long history of giving sick children everything they need."

Ava dabbed her eyes with a tissue. "Sick. I never thought I'd have to refer to one of my children as 'sick' before. It breaks my heart every time I hear that."

"I know, Ava, I know," Ellie said, with faux sympathy. "But, unfortunately, sick he is, and sick he most likely always will be." Ava seemed to flinch slightly every time Ellie used that descriptor, as, of course, she knew she would. "None of the psychiatrists who saw him here locally can explain what happened to him, so unfortunately we need to accept the fact that your son is...and I'm *so* sorry for having to be blunt about this...well, he's quite mad. His poor little psyche is broken, shattered, for some reason we can't begin to fathom."

Ellie watched happily as Ava began to cry harder and harder, her small mouth twisted into a cruel, satisfied smirk.

"But there is reason for a little hope, Ava," Ellie said, putting her hand on Ava's shoulder in equally faux compassion. "The psychiatrists at the Hopewell Institute are some of the very best in the country, many of them specializing in the treatment of insane children. If there is a team anywhere in the country who can figure a way to get your son out of his own broken mind, it will be them."

She patted Ava on the shoulder, then added in an off-handed way, "But, of course, regardless of what happens with that, he'll still be blind for the rest of his life." That caused Ava to cry even more forcefully, as Ellie had hoped it would.

"Now," Ellie said, reverting to her efficient bureaucrat mode. "Let's discuss the findings of the investigation."

Ava dried her eyes as she said, "OK, yes."

"So, I just want to confirm that your daughter is with her grandparents."

"Yes, in California. They came to get her right after we found Junior."

"Ah, yes," Ellie said, icily. "Fine. So, after doing a thorough investigation of the incident, we feel comfortable determining there is absolutely no finding of abuse."

Ava smiled wanly at that. "I knew there wouldn't be. There was no way I could believe for a second Adam could ever..."

"Oh, no, Ava," Ellie said, stopping her with an extended hand. "We weren't investigating Adam; we were investigating *you*. There's no finding of abuse against you."

Ava stared at Ellie for several seconds before laughing

once nervously, then said, "Me? Why would you have investigated me? I was in Boston when all this happened."

"Or so you claim," Ellie said. "Ava, Adam's statement is that he, Junior, and Sophie were playing in the backyard when Junior said he had to use the bathroom. He was gone for some time, and just when Adam thought he should check on the boy he heard you screaming, he came running to the attic to find you, alone, holding your son. You *claim* that you found him like that, but you would surely understand there were many in the unit that found that story...well, unlikely."

Ava's eyes widened as she seemed almost to gasp for air, puffing in a futile attempt to find the right words to answer Ellie.

"I spoke to Sophie in the presence of an advocate, and she confirmed Junior was there the whole time." (Which, Dear Friend, was an abject lie; she had simply added that detail to the documentation on her own. But the one truth to which any government bureaucracy cleaves is that once something has been documented by a government bureaucrat, it's now the truth.) "So, from this perspective, surely you can see where *you'd* be the one who came under suspicion, not Adam. Surely, as a fellow social worker, as an expert in childhood adversity, you can appreciate how problematic this all appears. Correct?"

Ava blanched slightly, dabbing her eyes lightly as she whispered in a defeated tone, "Yes...I suppose."

"But, as I said, there is no finding of abuse against you, so no need for this to be reported to your employers or to the licensing board," Ellie said. "Now, tomorrow, I'd like to speak to Adam at the house, *alone*. I called him earlier today and we're going to meet at three o'clock. I just want to tie up a few things before filing the final report."

Ava looked at Ellie, questioningly. "Alone? Why do you want to meet with him at the house alone?"

THE HOUSE ON BLACKSTONE HILL

Ellie's tone again changed, once more becoming stern. "Because, just as I am meeting with you alone now, there are some things I'd much rather discuss with him in private. Now, Ava, having made this request, it'd be considered...*suspicious*... if you should happen to be there or to show up in the hour or so that we'll be meeting. If that were to happen, we might have to reconsider these abuse findings. Is that clear?"

Ava's eyes narrowed at Ellie. "Yes," she said coolly. "It's perfectly clear."

They ended their meeting, and as Ellie walked Ava to the elevators, she reminded her not to be at the house in the afternoon. As Ellie smirked contemptuously at Ava and as the burnished steel doors of the elevators closed, the sigil branded on her skin again tingled hotly. She looked forward with great excitement to fulfilling her duty for the good of the coven.

[19]

OH, THAT FUCKING BITCH! AVA FUMED TO HERSELF AS SHE walked out of the DCF office. *Now I understand why people hate state social workers so much!*

She walked angrily to her car, thinking over the entire conversation with Ellie, the cool contempt with which the DCF worker appeared to hold her, the dismissive attitude about Ava's suffering, and the veiled threat she'd made at the end. Ava also felt like Ellie was intentionally choosing her words — though spoken in just the right tone of voice and crafted to sound as compassionate as possible — to hurt her as much as she could.

Sick, fucking twisted bitch!

Just as Ava was about to put her car in gear to go, her phone rang. Seeing that it was Donegal calling, she immediately answered.

"Hello, Patrick. How are you?"

"I'm very well, but the question is, how are you?"

Ava closed her eyes, wanting to vent angrily about everything that had just happened, but instead she chose to deep breathe the anger out instead of unloading everything on her friend. The surprisingly warm early June air smelled verdant as she breathed it in. "I'm as well as can be expected, Patrick. I'm hanging in there."

"Good. I'm glad to hear that. Please know that I'm constantly praying for you and your family and saying all my Rosaries in dedication to Junior."

"Thank you, Patrick," Ava said, feeling very tired suddenly by everything that had happened in her life the past two months. This meeting with Ellie was just the icing on a terrible cake. She also painfully realized how much she missed her Sophie. "I appreciate it."

"I'm sure you have a lot to do, so I just wanted to let you know that Father Villalobos has done some research and is ready to meet whenever you are. We can go into more detail later, but from what he said he'd like to visit the house as soon as possible. There are some pressing issues he'd like to discuss first, though. Are you free anytime soon?"

"Well," Ava said bitterly, "as it turns out, I need to vacate the house tomorrow afternoon, so we can meet at the Bittersweet Bakery for coffee if you want. Can we meet at three o'clock?"

"Sure. Father Villalobos is right here and says that's fine with him. Works for me, too. Why do you have to be out of the house, though?" Donegal asked, clearly confused.

Ava grunted. "Long story. I'll fill you in tomorrow."

[20]

AVA, ALWAYS HAVING BEEN ABLE TO FIND SMALL opportunities for humor even in the darkest moments in her life, felt like she was part of a joke when she and two priests walked into a café. After chatting for a while over some coffee and fresh pastries, however, Ava felt like she was in anything but a joke, with the humor long since left behind as the conversation settled down into the occult.

"So, Ava," Villalobos said, still chewing his biscotti, "Patrick has told me everything about your house, everything you've told him. He told me about the incident with the girl, the crying you heard, the drawing of the sigil, and, of course, what happened to your son."

Ava had cried so much the past two months she wondered how she still had any tears left, and though she desperately didn't want to weep anymore she again felt tears welling in her eyes at the mention of Junior. The urge to cry felt even stronger now that Villalobos seemed to be confirming her worst suspicions. "You...you think there's a connection between the two, between that...*thing* in my house and what happened to Junior?"

"I can all but guarantee it," he said reluctantly. "I've sadly seen this before. A sudden, unreasonable madness like that only comes from the evil of a demon."

Ava suddenly no longer felt like crying, she felt like fighting. She felt angry, a hot, burning rage that seemed to radiate back on itself because it had no real target. Ava wanted to tear that demon limb from limb, but knowing that wasn't possible made her feel weakly impotent and, in return, all the angrier.

"I've done some research on your house, Ava," Villalobos said. "You'd told Patrick that your husband had also done research before he bought the house. That's correct, right?"

"Yes, it is. He did."

The priests glanced at each other. "Did he share with you anything he found out or did you ever look anything up yourself?" Villalobos asked.

Ava thought for a moment, then shrugged her shoulders. "He said the house was old, an authentic colonial-era mansion. He said it'd burned down sometime in the 1600s, had passed from family to family, had been used by the British army for a while during the Revolution. I think he said it'd been an orphanage for some time in the 1800s. That's about all he mentioned, though. I didn't do any research myself because I was really busy at that time, going from the job at the college to the academy."

Villalobos looked at her for a time, his kind, dark brown eyes showing what looked like discomfort for what he had to say next. "Ava, I'm afraid it would seem that Adam deliberately kept much of the house's history from you. It's not hard to find online; it's very easy, in fact. Your house has a very long history of owners going mad, of servants being killed and tortured, of owners killing their entire families and then killing themselves."

"He...lied to me?" Ava said, her anger growing. "How

could he? I never would have agreed to move here if I had known about this."

"I don't believe," Villalobos said, "that he was acting completely of his own free will. Based upon what you told Patrick, the way you described it, I have to believe he was acting under some influence of the demon even then. That's not to defend his actions, it's just to let you know that it appears your husband hasn't been entirely himself since even before you moved into the house."

Ava's eyes widened with fright as she brought a hand to her mouth. "You mean...he's possessed?!"

"No, I don't, actually," Villalobos said, sipping coffee. "I think he's what we'd call 'obsessed,' which is a diabolical mental focus, different than possession though it's source is still demonic. That means that the demon is in his mind, whispering foul, vile lies to him, perhaps making him hallucinate, so the decisions he's been making haven't been his own."

"I don't understand how that can be. He seems so normal. After what happened to Junior, he was so caring...so compassionate."

"Like I said, Ava, *some* things he's been doing haven't been entirely of his own free will, so it's possible that once the demon lets go of his mind for a time, he's just his normal self. He might honestly not even remember the times he's been obsessed by the demon."

Ava looked out the window sadly, feeling much as she did during her conversation with Donegal on Good Friday. Just too much information, too bizarre for her to manage all at once, just entirely too much. Ava felt tired, so very tired these past two months. Although she knew part of it was the final few weeks of pregnancy, most of it started with that conversation in Donegal's office and everything that had transpired since then. Ava was desperately tired, but now she was also angrier than she'd ever been before in her entire life. Angry, and feeling a great need to protect her people. She wanted her family to be safe once again.

"So...we need to exorcise the house and save my husband," she said, at last, looking at Villalobos. "Where do we begin?"

Donegal smiled. "See?" he said, "I told you she was feisty."

Villalobos chuckled, and said, "Yes, I can see that, which is good. But we're not there, not yet. Despite popular opinion and what the movies show, we don't rush in with crucifixes a-blazing every time there might be a demon involved. Most of the time we actually try to find reasons for it to *not* be a demon, and there usually has to be a pretty lengthy investigation, but under these circumstances that'll be expedited."

"OK," Ava said. "So, what are we doing?"

"I need to go to the house to get a feel of what we're dealing with," Villalobos said. "I'd also like to talk to Adam about what's going on. You said you haven't told him anything yet, about talking to us, talking about the house. Right?"

"Yes, that's right."

"Fine. Then that's where we'll begin. Let's go to your house so I can look around, gather some data, and then speak to Adam."

"Well," Ava said, looking at her watch, "it's now four o'clock, so that sweet young lady from DCF should be gone by now. Even if she isn't, she said to give her about an hour, so I think I'm good."

"Alright then," Donegal said. "You lead the way and we will follow in my car."

As Ava took the short drive between the café and her home on the hill, she fought between feeling hopeful, feeling melancholic, and feeling so angry she wanted to personally fight that demon and make it pay for what it had done to her family. Between those three vacillating emotions, Ava mostly felt like fighting.

[21]

Adam sat on the steps of his portico awaiting Ellie's arrival, the warm air enveloping him. Though she'd called to formally schedule this appointment, that had largely been unnecessary. His instructions and expectations had been whispered to him, and he knew Ellie's coven had given her directions as well. Both knew exactly what they had to do.

Since he had broken on that day he'd attacked Junior, Adam had given up any pretenses of resistance. He was now wholly dedicated to the demon, a willing servant, and felt fully satisfied with that dedication. When around Ava he intentionally put on an act, almost like he was wearing a mask of the former Adam. He was sympathetic, hugging Ava and gently kissing her head as she cried about the terrible trauma that had occurred to their son; all the while Adam delighted in the cruel sacrifice he'd made to Andromelech. He would check in with Ava, asking after her emotions, seeing to her needs; all the while he was aching for the next sacrifice he'd soon be able to offer. He was, to all outward appearances, Adam as he'd always been.

However, that old Adam was lost forever.

As he looked back on that Adam now, he thought how weak he was, how effete, how pathetic. He loathed that Adam, very pleased to have killed him utterly, thereby allowing this new man to come forward fully. Adam eagerly looked forward to where this new life, this new Adam, was going to take him.

His reverie about the past and future Adams was broken when he heard a car swiftly coming up his driveway. Adam watched as an oversized black SUV with state plates pulled up and a petite young woman clambered out of it. He looked at Ellie now as she paused, smiling, hand on hip, giving him time to drink in her appeal.

He saw she was short, something he'd always found quite appealing, with large, firm breasts, something he found even more appealing. Her pale, milky-white skin made her bright red, pouty lips look even more brilliant. Her dark hair was done up in a tight bun, which, as he watched her hungrily, she reached up to release, allowing her hair to tumble down past her shoulders. Ellie took off her glasses and undid the first two buttons of her blouse, looking at Adam seductively as she did so.

Adam stood and said nothing, as nothing needed to be said. He went into the house, Ellie dutifully following, and led her to the rear cellar room. It was exactly as he knew it would be, red drapes on the walls, black candles burning in corner iron candelabras, the heat from the many flames intense. The stone altar was unadorned.

Turning on each other, they began to kiss passionately, like lovers achingly separated for entirely too long. They fell on each other not merely passionately, but violently, as clothes were removed not patiently or carefully, but rather ripped from their bodies. They kissed, their hands roaming over each other's naked bodies, touching, squeezing, pinching, playing. Ellie took Adam's face in her hands, something that could normally be considered sweet and loving, but instead, she used the opportunity to bite Adam's lower lip as she kissed him. The pain made him flinch, yet Ellie held his head in place, so he pulled away forcefully from her teeth. This ripped his lip, and he tasted his own blood. Surprised yet aroused by this violence, Adam responded by slapping Ellie's face hard.

As her head turned slowly back towards his, her dark hair thrown crazily across her face, he could see her smiling mouth had blood oozing out of it, her eyes blazing at him even more hungrily than before. Her contented and satisfied sigh at being struck was all he could take, and, as she licked the blood off her lips, Adam lifted her onto the altar so he could finally take her.

He slid into her easily, twisting Ellie's arms behind her as she did. Adam kissed her bloody lips, his mouth trailing towards her neck and shoulders, biting her soft, milky flesh hard enough to leave deep marks. The violence was delicious, and Adam pummeled Ellie's petite body as hard as he could. He let go of her arms so he could grab her ass, pulling Ellie towards him as he thrust forward to increase the impact. As he did, Ellie raked her long nails across Adam's back, leaving deep gouges in it, trailing off thin slices of skin.

The pain intensified their pleasure, blood mixing freely with the sweat that now covered their heaving bodies.

Adam pulled out of Ellie suddenly, turning her around roughly and bending her over the altar. Pulling back on her arms he again slid right into her, continuing the machine-like pounding her was giving her. Adam let go of Ellie's wrists after some time so he could grab her dark hair, twisting it tightly into his fist as he pulled her head back, forcing her to push up her ass and arch her back. In so doing she also exposed her throat.

As he did so, Adam smelled the odor of burnt flesh, just as

ANTONIO RICARDO SCOZZE

he knew he would. He continued to thrust into her frantically for a few minutes more, feeling that delicious pressure building deep inside him. As the inevitable swiftly approached, Adam reached out his right hand, hearing the sound of crispy burnt skin rasping as the dagger was placed into it.

Swelling inside of Ellie as she fervently whispered, "Hail Satan," Adam drew the razor-sharp blade across her throat hard even as he started to fill her womb with his seed. A look of horrified shock and surprise was etched on her face as, with every explosive squirt inside of Ellie, Adam would saw the blade deeper into her neck, making her blood squirt all over the altar. Her body went limp as Adam stopped sawing, having cut all the way to her spine.

He easily pushed her dead body onto the altar, panting heavily, feeling satisfied and refreshed. Her naked body was even paler now that so much of her blood had been drained out of it. A look of surprise and horror was permanently etched on her Ellie's face, her wide-open, dead eyes already glazing over. This assignment did not end the way she thought it would, nor the way she was told it would.

As Adam looked at his bloody sacrifice, he reached into Ellie's neck to scoop up some of her still-warm blood and smeared it all over his face.

At that moment, Adam could feel it. He could feel *him*. He could feel Andromelech swell with power, with delight, with delicious pleasure at the death, horror, and evil he'd been able to make Adam do willingly in his name. Adam was pleased to have satisfied his master.

In the very next moment, Adam was shown a vision. Not a vision of historical violence or temptations of harming his family; those, together with the whispers, had altogether ended the day he gave himself over to the demon. This was a vision of something currently happening somewhere else,

180

knowledge being shared by Andromelech with a good and faithful servant.

Where once was Ellie's dead body sprawled across the stone altar, he now saw Ava with two men inside a cozy, comfortable café. He recognized it as the Bittersweet Bakery in Deerfield, and he also knew the one man to be Ava's former colleague, that priest Donegal. The other man, the young one with thick, black hair, mocha-toned skin, and a square jaw, he did not know. He could see that the other man, however, was also a priest.

Then, like a searching radio that suddenly finds a station, he heard their conversation.

"I need to go to the house to get a feel of what we're dealing with," the Mexican-accented priest said. "I'd also like to talk to Adam about what's going on. You said you haven't told him anything yet, about talking to us, talking about the house. Right?"

You want to talk to me? I'll fucking shove a crucifix down your throat first, buddy.

"Yes, that's right," Ava said.

Oh, Ava, you lying cunt.

"Fine. Then that's where we'll begin. Let's go to your house so I can look around, gather some data, and then speak to Adam."

"Well, it's four o'clock, so that sweet young lady from DCF should be gone by now. Even if she isn't, she said to give her about an hour, so I think I'm good."

Yeah, she's gone alright...you're good.

"Alright then," Donegal said. "You lead the way and we will follow in my car."

They're leaving now, Adam thought. *They'll be here soon.*

Still clutching the bloody dagger, Adam smiled wickedly and thought. *Fine, let them come. I'll be ready for them when they get here.*

[22]

"OH, BOY," AVA SAID TO THE PRIESTS WHEN THEY JOINED her in front of her house, pointing to the state SUV. "I hope this doesn't mean trouble for me."

"Oh, I'm sure it'll be fine," Donegal said. "We can certainly vouch for you if there are any issues." Ava felt unsettled but approached her home with the priests, nonetheless.

"Can you feel it, Patrick?" Villalobos whispered. "Can you feel its evil...its hatred?"

"Yes, I can. I certainly can."

Ava opened the door, and as soon as they entered, the trio was met with foul odors and a thick, humid, stuffy air like nothing Ava had ever felt before. Her entire house reeked of rotting flesh, sulfur, blood, and burnt meat.

Ava, retching at these new, disgusting odors, said to the priests, "It's never smelled like this before, and the air has never been this thick before. What the hell is happening?"

She looked over at the pair of priests and was concerned to see they looked as horrified as she felt, terror clearly etched on both their faces as each clutched their crucifixes.

Perhaps instinctively, perhaps as a deliberate ward against the overpowering evil they felt, Donegal and Villalobos almost simultaneously made the sign of the cross.

And as soon as they did, the three of them heard a loud shriek, a howl that was unearthly and impossible, coming from everywhere all at once, surrounding them, almost drowning them in its power. It was a shriek of pain, horror, and rage all at once, and seemed to almost be coming from the house itself, from the walls, the floors, even from the very hill upon which the house stood. It was the sound of loathsome evil itself.

Villalobos, who was holding his crucifix outward like a shield, took some steps forward into the foyer to join Ava there as the demonic shriek continued, then said, "I've never felt a power like this before. Never dealt with a demon this powerful, this evil. Ava, I don't think there's anything I can do today against this beast. I'm sorry, but we need to leave so I can consult with the Vatican. This thing is simply too powerful for me to handle alone."

Ava was about to respond to him, when she suddenly heard what sounded like bare feet running followed by a human shriek that replaced the demonic one. To her shock and horror, she turned to see some red-faced beast had leaped onto Donegal and clung tenaciously to his back as it stabbed him with a dagger, thrusting the blade repeatedly deep into her friend's belly. His eyes wide with pain and fear, Donegal stumbled forward and fell, blood pouring from his wounds and wrenching the blade from his attacker's hand as he did.

As he loomed over Donegal's body, Ava realized with horror that the red-faced beast was Adam, naked, smeared with blood all over his face. Moving with a speed and agility she did not know he was capable of, Adam rushed Villalobos, striking him in the head with a fire iron he'd had clutched in his teeth while attacking Donegal. Adam hit the priest hard, smashing his head with a loud crack, and Villalobos immediately crumpled, falling to the floor.

Then, having dispatched the priests with ease, Adam dropped the fire poker with a loud clang and calmly retrieved the dagger. He turned to Ava, slowly approaching his backpedaling, terrified wife.

"Hello, darling," Adam said, eyes madly wide open, clearly quite insane. "It's so good to see you."

Ava's mind raced, trying to desperately grasp the trauma she was witnessing.

"However, my dear," Adam went on. "I take serious offense at you bringing men into my house without my knowledge. How are we ever supposed to have an open, honest relationship if you're fucking men in my house *BEHIND MY BACK?!*" he screamed. "I am not my father. *I AM NOT MY FATHER!!*"

"No...no-no-no...it's...it's not like that," Ava said, holding her hands out to keep Adam away as still she slowly backed away from him. "We just wanted...we wanted to talk...to talk to you..."

"There is no talking now, Ava," Adam said, now tittering manically as he did. "There's nothing left to say. See, here's the thing. Bad news for you, we're kind of done. Sorry, not sorry. I belong now to Andromelech, and I do what he tells me to."

"But..." Ava stammered weakly, backpedaling. "I'm here to save you."

"*SAVE ME?!*" Adam bellowed loudly, angrily, then laughed maniacally. "I don't *need* to be saved...I've found my savior."

Ava was about to plead with her husband for sanity, for mercy, for him to come to his senses, when her legs gave out, weakened by the utter horror she'd seen. She now pushed herself back, crawling away from this monster her husband had become as he slowly approached her, trying to form words, but unable to as her mind raced, and she gasped for breath.

"See, originally, I was told all I'd have to do is kill some random woman, and he'd be happy, he'd be satisfied, and I'd get what I wanted. But, wouldn't you know it? Turns out he's a bit more demanding, and at first, what Andromelech wanted was Junior, so I gave our son over to him. Now what he wants, what he *NEEDS*, Ava, is that fucking baby inside you..."

Ava, hyperventilating with horror, too weak, too overcome with fear to push herself back anymore, froze in place on the marble floor. Adam approached, getting closer and closer, the bloody blade poised to strike, his maniacal laughter increasing with intensity, his voice rising to a rage as he screamed angrily.

"We'd wanted you to give birth and then sacrifice him properly, but you just had to fuck that up, *DIDN'T YOU?!*" Adam shrieked at his wife, then laughed.

And he stepped closer, closer...

"*DIDN'T YOU?!!* You just had to fuck up *EVERYTHING*, don't you, cunt?! So, unfortunately, now I'm just going to have to cut that fucking thing out of your belly! Aw, too bad, so sad, bye-bye..."

Closer, closer, until he finally stood, towering over his prone and terrified wife. All he had to do was plunge the dagger down and Ava would be dead.

"Well, my beloved, you won't fuck this up. Now, please, try not to move, because this is going to be very, *very* painful," he said, smiling cruelly at Ava.

Adam pulled the dagger back to strike down into Ava with all his force, his mouth pulled back into a toothy grimace that looked like a silent snarl, blue eyes blazing madly around the dried and flaking blood smeared on his face...

[23]

AND IN THAT MOMENT, IN THAT HALF-SECOND MOMENT AS Adam raised the dagger, Ava saw one brief chance to free herself, and she took it.

She had seen that Adam, as he stalked towards her, had foolishly stepped well within the reach of her legs. Drawing on the last shreds of her remaining strength, Ava forcefully pulled her knee up as close to her chest as she could and kicked out as hard as possible squarely against Adam's exposed knee. Though only wearing sneakers, Ava was able to stomp his knee backward with great force, smashing it painfully.

Adam howled in agony as he fell to the floor, writhing. Ava wasted no time and quickly stood, feeling a surge of power and energy as soon as she kicked out Adam's knee, intent on running out of that house as fast as possible. She wheeled around because the rear French doors were the closest exit for her, and was prepared to run as fast as she ever had in her life – only to see with horrified disgust what appeared to be a man burnt to a blackened crisp, smoke floating up off his immolated body, green eyes staring lidless at her. He stood in front of the doors silently blocking her way.

Ava screamed in horror, her mind struggling to remain sane. She looked at the front door, but to get there she'd have to pass by Adam, and though he remained writhing on the floor, screaming threats and insults at her, she didn't want to go anywhere near him since he still grasped the dagger.

Looking back quickly at the burnt man, who hadn't moved towards her, Ava saw she could get to the cellar quickly without passing near Adam. She knew there was a door leading outside through one of the side rooms down there, which seemed like her only option. Ava ran the few paces it took her to get there, noting that the burnt man merely tracked her movements with his eyes, not moving to stop her.

At the top of the steps Ava flicked on the lights, but now they didn't turn on at all. "*FUCK!*" she screamed in frustration and terror. Looking down into the inky blackness of the cellar, she realized she could see a soft orange glow coming from somewhere down there. Dreading what that might be in the dark cellar, yet fearing a bloody death at the hands of her deranged husband even more, Ava plunged into the shadowy basement...

[24]

"*I HATE YOU!*" ADAM SCREAMED ANGRILY AT THIS WIFE as she ran to the cellar door. "*I FUCKING HATE YOU! I'M GOING TO KILL YOU, YOU FUCKING BITCH!!*"

Adam writhed in pain, feeling an overwhelming fear that she was going to get away, his mind racing with ways to interdict her escape, yet also feeling impotent to stop her. He knew what he was expected to do, he dreaded the thought of failure, he just didn't know how to make that happen. Adam lay there, writhing still, not knowing what to do, when he smelled the delicious odor of burnt spices.

"Get up," he heard Andromelech whisper demandingly.

"I...I can't," Adam pleaded through the intense pain. "She...she kicked out..."

"*GET UP!!*" the demon now roared, so loudly that the entire house shook. He swept one gloved hand upwards, which pulled Adam swiftly to his feet. As he stood now for the first time since being kicked by Ava, the pain he felt in his knee was so intense he felt queasy and dizzy, and feared he might pass out. He stood awkwardly, favoring his right leg heavily over his injured left one, the knee swollen magnificently.

"Do not fail me again, Man," Andromelech whispered to Adam...

[25]

AVA SLOWLY WORKED HER WAY DOWN THE DARKENED cellar steps, wanting to run but tempering her speed, feeling the walls to help her stay safe. The last thing she wanted was to tumble down the stairs, breaking bones, waiting helplessly for Adam – or God only knew what else – to find her and rip her baby from her womb.

As she carefully descended the stairs, Ava could hear Adam talking, then the words "get up" loudly roared as even the earth beneath her seemed to tremble. Ava had no idea what was going on up there, but she felt confident she'd better get out as quickly as possible.

Ava finally made it safely into the darkened cellar, seeing that there was indeed an orange glow coming from the rear room with the stone table. Ava rarely went down to the basement, so she wasn't certain which room had the door leading outside. With her heart racing and her breath coming in panicked gulps, her mind flying with possible escape routes to safety and survival, it was even harder for her to focus enough to recall which room it was. She was fairly certain it wasn't the softly illuminated rear one, but her brain was so confused with terror that it might've been.

Ava walked down the hallway as quickly as she safely could in the dark, running her hand along the wall to help her find the storage room with the door to escape this nightmare. As she did, she felt the door jamb of the first room and then found the knob. Ava opened the door and suddenly saw a brightly illuminated room, sun pouring in through high windows. Though brick-walled and floored, Ava stared in at shocked disbelief as she realized she was looking into a room that was not physically the room behind this door.

Ava stood there staring, mouth hanging gaping open in shocked surprise, as she realized there were two people in this room. One was a man, dressed in what looked to be clothing from the 1600s, behind a naked girl with chocolate brown skin. The girl was painfully secured to a strapado as the man pulled her hair back and cruelly raped her. Both looked directly at her, repeating, "You're next, Ava," in ghostly whispers, devoid of any life or feeling.

She stood there in frozen, shocked silence as the pair intoned this phrase over and over again, the man pounding her with increasing intensity. The pair continued to look at her and repeat that threat, even as the man drew a blade across the girl's throat and as blood poured from her severed neck. Despite a neck sliced open, despite the blood squirting out viciously, still the girl repeated those words in a harsh whisper together with her killer.

"You're next, Ava... You're next, Ava... You're next, Ava..."

The door closed with a loud slam, plunging Ava back into the dark. She stood there completely still, immobilized by sanity-snapping terror, as she felt her heart pound in her chest and heard nothing but her own shallow, panicked breathing in the blackness.

I have to find that door to the outside, she told herself as she turned, not wanting to see what was in any more rooms but knowing she had no other alternatives. *I have to.*

She opened the next door, and again saw a room that was not physically there, one that *could not* physically be there. It was one of the second-floor bedrooms, illuminated by gas lamps. In it stood a tweed-suited portly man, salt-and-pepper beard, holding an ax. Before him, facing Ava, knelt the girl whose ghost she had seen, in the nightie she'd been wearing on that day.

Just as the first pair had done, they looked at Ava as they almost chanted, "You're next, Ava...You're next, Ava..."

Then, with a whooshing arc, the man swung the ax down into the girl's head, chopping deep into her skull with a dull *thunk!* She fell to the floor, blood pouring out all over the wooden planks of the bedroom, and again and again, the man chopped down into her smashed head. Yet all the while they both continued to repeat "You're next, Ava," the girl doing so even after there wasn't enough of her mouth to speak clearly, so instead she just gurgled loudly. Her one, still pristine eye stared uselessly at Ava until again the door closed of its own accord with another loud slam.

Oh my God, oh my God, oh my God! Ava now thought, fear quickly rising to panic. *I can't do this, I can't do this! But I have to find that fucking door to get out of here!*

Ava told herself she could only manage the horror of one more room, so she slid down the hall as swiftly as she could until once again feeling her way to the next doorknob. She opened it, and again saw something that was impossible. Through the door, she saw the outside of her house in the cool dawn, as a middle-aged, gray-haired woman slowly tortured an olive-skinned young girl by slowly slicing off long strips of her skin.

"You're next, Ava...You're next, Ava...You're next, Ava,"

they, too, intoned in their dead, ghostly whispers, until the door once again slammed in her face.

Panting, terrified, confused, Ava looked down the hall, seeing that there was soft candlelight coming from the rear room. She also saw that it appeared to be perfectly normal, though the walls looked red for some reason. Ava figured, with growing dread, that she'd have to go the rear room and take her chances with what she found there, as there clearly was no making it through any other room. She took a deep breath, let it out slowly, steeling herself for what fresh horror awaited her, and strode towards the rear room...

[26]

"She's in the cellar," Andromelech whispered to Adam, "at the altar. Go to her and make the sacrifice. Kill her slowly and give me that child." Then, just as suddenly as the demon appeared, he was gone.

Adam stood in the foyer, the pain in his knee throbbing so intensely he feared he might vomit. He took one step towards the cellar door, but he was barely able to support any weight on his shattered knee. That, however, was irrelevant; he'd been given directions from Andromelech, and he could not fail. Adam staggered forward carefully, putting as little weight on his left leg as he could; he'd bring up his right leg as quickly as possible, dragging his injured one behind.

Adam made his way to the cellar door as fast as he could with his shattered knee, then peered into the deep dark of the cellar. He took the first step carefully by supporting his weight on the handrails, then hopped down. The first step echoed loudly as he landed, followed by another slow, laborious hop, and then a third.

His mind shattered by the demon's evil, the pain

tormenting him, Adam screamed out to Ava, "*COME OUT, COME OUT, WHEREVER YOU ARE!!*" as he hopped down to step four, and then five.

Then, about half-way down, he heard her...

[27]

AVA WALKED INTO THE REAR ROOM CLOSING THE DOOR over behind her, and immediately saw the naked, bloody body of a woman sprawled out on the stone table. She clapped her hand over her mouth to stifle the scream that bubbled up in her throat as she saw that the woman's throat was slashed open, blood having gushed out all over the table and her chest. As Ava took one tenuous, disgusted step closer, she suddenly realized it was Ellie, the twisted DCF worker.

At just that moment she whirled as she heard a loud *THUD!* as Adam made his first awkward, loud hopping step down the stairs, painfully making his way down to where she was. Ava had hoped she'd completely immobilized him, yet obviously she had not.

THUD! The second step.

She looked around, trying desperately to find somewhere to hide, but there was none.

THUD! The third step.

Ava looked to see if there was anything she could use as a weapon. Finding none, her mind then raced as she wondered if perhaps she'd be able to rush him in the dark hall, push past him as hard as she could, possibly knocking him down in the process because of his knee. If she could do that, Ava figured she could quickly make her way out the front door – so long as she didn't get stabbed or slashed in the process. *It's worth a try!* she thought as she tried very hard not to wonder if there would be any new horrors guarding doorways up there.

THUD! The fourth step.

"COME OUT, COME OUT, WHEREVER YOU ARE!!" she heard him shriek from the steps, the madness in his mind expressed loudly in his voice.

Just as Ava was preparing herself for the desperate run down the hall, steeling herself for what could possibly lead to her own death as much as it could lead to her safety, she heard a soft rustling behind her and saw something move in the corner of her eye. She turned, and there she saw Ellie's corpse standing behind her, the entirety of her eyes now nothing but glistening black orbs. Ava's eyes widened, and she was about to scream when Ellie's dead hand shot out and grabbed hold of her throat like a vice, shutting off any screams and most of her air.

Then, with a strength she never would have been capable of in life, Ellie's corpse whirled Ava around so she again faced the door, her right hand clutching her throat tightly from behind, her left arm woven between Ava's, keeping both of her arms immobile in an icy grip that was like being held by a marble statue. Ava tried to break free, but the power that reanimated Ellie's corpse had clearly also given her impossible strength. Ava could go nowhere.

The Ellie corpse then made an inhuman, high-pitched screech, something that sounded like two pieces of metal being slid against each other, mixed together with deep roar.

Ava stared at the door, trapped and unable to escape, awaiting her fate...

Adam made his way down the steps as swiftly as he could after he heard the Ellie corpse screech, but he also knew that Ava had nowhere to go. She was trapped. So, knowing that implacable fact, he decided to have some cruel fun, taunting her as her death approached.

Once in the hallway, Adam again cried out, "*COME OUT, COME OUT, WHEREVER YOU ARE!!*" as if they were playing a fun game of hide-and-seek. "*I WONDER WHERE SHE COULD BE?!*" he yelled tauntingly, as he loudly opened the door to the first storage room. The door banged open, revealing nothing but an empty room, save for a few of their boxes.

"*NOPE, SHE'S NOT IN THERE!!*" he again bellowed. "*WHERE COULD SHE BE?!!*"

Adam played this sadistic jape with her all the way down the hall, his injured walk making a step-slide sound every time he lurched forward. He teased her as he made his way down the hall as if he truly didn't know where she was, swinging open each door down the hall, then wondering loudly where she could possibly be.

Then, he at last came to the closed door of the rear room, where he knew Ava awaited him clutched in the immovable grip of the Ellie corpse...

.

[29]

AVA SQUIRMED IN THE OBDURATE GRASP OF ELLIE'S CORPSE, trying to break free as she heard her husband inching his way closer, his taunts obviously an attempt to heighten her terror and dread of the inevitable. It was working.

She could hear him getting closer with the weird sound of his dragging leg after each normal step, the sound of the storeroom doors banging open, only to have him predictably note that Ava was not, in fact, in that room, and to query loudly where she might be. If not for the deadly intent behind his slow movement towards her, his game would be ridiculous.

Ava had heard his step-slide getting closer, each door that banged open getting nearer and nearer until finally, she knew he was standing, wordless, just outside the door of the rear room. After all the crashing and yelling he had done making his way toward her, Ava now found this deathly silence even more terrifying, and she could feel the blood throbbing in her veins. Ava was so filled with horror she feared she might black out.

Then, snapping her consciousness back fully, Ava heard

Adam hiss a whisper from just outside the door, "*Are you in heeeeeeeeere, Ava?*" Adam slowly pushed the door open, making the creaking sound of the door seem to last an eternity, and then he stepped in.

At that moment, Ava realized her husband was gone forever as she saw how beastly he'd become. He was hunched over from the effort of walking with a shattered knee, his sweat-slicked naked body glistening in the soft orange glow of the candles. His legs were twisted at a weird angle as he tried to favor his good right leg, and his hands were before him, one clutching the dagger, making him look strangely insect-like. Adam's face was contorted in pain, rage, and insanity, still streaked with the blood that Ava assumed came from the corpse now holding her immovable.

His blue eyes burned with intensity as he looked at Ava, and at last said, "Oh, there you are."

He slowly shambled his way towards her, saying between snickering, "Now, Ava, darling, that was a very naughty thing you did up there. Very naughty, indeed. It hurt, *a lot*, and you almost got away...we can't have *that*, can we?"

Adam was now upon her, and gently slid the cold steel of the blade all along her face, her neck, over the swell of her breasts. "Doing that was also quite a stupid thing, I must say, *Doctor* Rosenburg-Long. See, because whereas before I just would've just stabbed you in the heart or something, just killed you really quickly, then cut that baby out of you, now I have to kill you *slooooooooooowly*, with as much pain as possible."

As Adam said this, he flicked the blade quickly across Ava's cheek just below her eye, slicing into her face. She moaned in pain, but little sound was made due to the Ellie corpse's grip on her throat.

"Oh, I'm sorry, what was that?" Adam said, cupping his ear and leaning in towards his wife. "What? That hurt? Yeah,

I fucking know that hurt, you dumb cunt. Try getting kicked in the knee sometime." The dagger flicked again, giving Ava a matching slash on the other cheek.

"I think that looks much better," Adam said. Then, looking at the corpse, he said, "Don't you agree, Ellie?" Ellie stared at him mutely, her black-orbed eyes offering no comprehension at all. "Hmm...I'll take your silence as agreement."

Adam then pressed the dagger to Ava's forehead hard and slowly sliced it across her flesh, cutting so deeply Ava could hear the blade grind into her skull, hot blood pouring down over her face. She writhed in pain, trying to get away from Adam's torment, but the Ellie corpse's grip was obdurate.

Adam approached Ava and said, "*He* tells me I have to kill you slowly, with lots of pain, and much blood. And right now, with my knee hurting like it does, I'm thinking I'm totally OK with that!" Adam leaned in close to his wife then, whispering, as he said, "But then...then, at the very end, just before you die, I'm going to cut this little fucker out of you, and give him over to Andromelech to consume, and I'll make sure you live long enough to fucking see it."

Adam stood back from his wife, viewing her as an artist might view a blank canvass, then tore off her light summer blouse and bra to violently expose her chest. "Where to begin, where to begin?" Adam asked, even as he gave her a few quick, shallow cuts on her breasts, just as he had to her cheeks. He then put the dagger point against her shoulder, and said, "Here's what I'm going to do. I'm going to slowly slide this dagger into your shoulder, and you're going to feel it as it cuts into tendons, slices ligaments, and..."

At that moment Adam's tirade was interrupted by Ellie's corpse suddenly screeching again, but this one sounded somehow different than the first. It sounded strangely pained, almost desperate. Adam looked up at her and saw her black eyes were turned towards the door, but before he could pivot to see what was there, the fire poker came smashing down on his head, making a crack and a wet *thwock!* sound as it connected with him. He immediately fell to the ground hard, revealing to Ava the panting, bleeding image of Father Villalobos.

The Ellie corpse let go of Ava now as she seemed repulsed by the priest's crucifix, almost as if she were physically pained by it. She turned her blanched face away from it and waved her hands wildly to block her view, still screeching loudly as she did. Looking down, Villalobos saw the dagger on the ground near Adam and picked it up, then pounced on the cowering corpse and used the dagger to finish off the decapitation started by Adam. The screeching immediately ended, and Ellie Sanders fell to the floor, dead once again.

Villalobos dropped Ellie's head to the floor and took off his black priest's coat to cover Ava's nakedness. "Let's get out of here! Now!" he said.

"We need..." Ava said, as her throat ached painfully and she had trouble speaking above a harsh whisper because of Ellie's grip on her, "We need...to get...Donegal."

"Yes, you're right. Let's go!"

The pair ran up the cellar stairs to the foyer and were surprised, though thrilled, to see that Donegal still barely clung to life. Each of them grabbed a wrist and together they dragged him out of that house to the warm June day, and to safety, that awaited them outside...

[30]

Adam awoke slowly, groggily, sometime later. Villalobos had hit Adam as hard as possible over the top of his head, cracking his skull and concussing him terribly. Adam's mind swam as if he were drunk, his vision was blurry, and his head throbbed as painfully as his knee. He looked around from the cold brick floor, confused, trying to piece together what had happened.

Then, in a sudden, everything came rushing back to him, the horrifying fear of failure striking him like an icicle to his heart.

"Ava?!" he cried, whirling his head from side to side on the floor, neither seeing nor hearing anything. "AVA?! *WHERE ARE YOU?!!*

Adam slowly pulled himself to his feet using the bloody altar for support, then, standing in the rear room, pivoted from one side to the next, calling out for his wife in a panicked tone, "AVA!! WHERE ARE YOU?! *COME BACK HERE!!"*

He stood there, dumbfounded and spinning in place, not

knowing what to do or which way to go, but only knowing he had to do something or else — and then, mid-pivot, Andromelech suddenly stood before him.

The demon stood there, resplendent as always. He wore a tight, all white suit that clung to his lean body, the jacket of which had garish tails. Atop his head he wore a black fedora with an overly large brim, a white silk band going around it that matched his white silk cravat, several peacock feathers gaudily stuck into it.

Andromelech raised a black-gloved hand and pointed at Adam. "You have failed me, Man. She is gone. She has already called for help. You have failed me...again."

Adam, feeling the full weight of his failure, together with a painfully throbbing head and an aching knee, closed his eyes in exhaustion, shame, pain, and fear. When he opened them again, the demon still stood before him, but now his hands were extended, handing something to Adam.

He looked down and saw Andromelech was handing him an ax.

"You know what to do," the demon whispered.

Adam stared at the ax and began to titter again madly as he did so. He then took it from the demon's hands, his eyes racing all over the room, looking around madly, a twisted smile spreading widely across his face. He laughed more and more loudly, more freely, more insanely.

Adam turned the ax in his hands, so the sharp blade of the head faced him, and in one swift movement chopped it into his own face. His first blow struck, slicing through his nose, angled so that it obliterated his left eye, and yet he merely laughed louder and louder as the blood poured down his face, his chest, dribbling on the floor.

As Adam did, Andromelech stood nearby, watching lustfully.

Adam pulled back and chopped into his own face again, smashing into his mouth and shattering his teeth, yet still, he laughed, a laugh that was quickly turning into a thick gurgling sound wet with blood. Then, again he chopped, this time deep into his own forehead, the blood now pouring out of his head, flowing down his body in many swift rivulets.

He pulled back, again and again and again chopping the blood-drenched ax into his own face, smashing it into a sloppy, bloody mess, something unrecognizable as once being human. Still, he gurgle-laughed, chopping what was once his face into an utterly ruined mess, save for one pristine, bright blue eye that stared out of the red mash that was once his face.

Adam suddenly stopped, that single eye looking around, his mind freed for one brief moment from the demon's tyranny, and in that moment realized all the shocking evil he had been responsible for.

With a mouth almost too shattered to work, and a throat choked with blood, still he said in a sloppy gurgle, "What have I done?"

Then, enslaved by Andromelech again just that quickly, Adam smashed away at his face with increased furor and violence, chopping far into his face until finally, the ax lodged deeply into his brain. His arms fell limply to his side, he teetered there, standing for one moment longer, and then suddenly collapsed, dead.

Andromelech had stood there the entire time, watching Adam destroy his own face, smiling more and more as the bloody violence progressed. Now, raising his arms, the demon absorbed all the hate, the pain, the evil that he'd created, almost as if he were breathing in a pleasing odor, and he was well pleased. Laughing triumphantly, Andromelech raised his arms further, as flames burst out spontaneously throughout the entire house, every surface immediately engulfed in flames. Adam's and Ellie's bodies, the walls, floors, Adam's computer and almost-done manuscript – everything in the house took to flame in an instant.

And all the while, the demon Andromelech laughed happily.

[31]

AVA AND VILLALOBOS DRAGGED DONEGAL WELL SAFE OF the house, almost all the way to where the driveway began its turn towards the corkscrew down the hill. As Ava called the police, Villalobos heard Donegal's final confession. Ava, crying bitter tears of anguish, held his hand tightly in hers as his breathing slowed and, after letting out one last, long breath, his body relaxed. She then gently closed his eyes after her beloved friend died.

She and Villalobos sat, exhausted, terrified, staring at the house. The priest had given her a handkerchief for her wounds, which she pressed tightly to her heavily bleeding forehead cut. As they sat there waiting for help to arrive, after a time the entire house burst into flames as if every inch had been doused in gasoline and a match had been put to it. All the windows burst apart as the flames shot out, the fire quickly spreading throughout it. The ancient wood, desiccated by three centuries of use, quickly burned, the fire spreading to the very core of the house. Flames swiftly ripped through the slate-shingled roof, shooting high into the sky.

Ava knew her husband's body was somewhere in there,

but she also knew that's all it was now. The *body* of her husband, a man who had died long ago. As Ava sat there and thought on it, she believed he'd actually died that day when first he ran up this hill, drawn to the house even then by the power of the demon.

The flames, growing hotter and higher, raged with wild intensity. Then, over the roar and crackling of the flames, Ava heard a deep, demonic, yet delighted laughter. It was over the sound of the flames, yet somehow seemed to be part of them, perhaps even in the flames.

Ava and Villalobos looked at each other, both hearing the demon laugh.

"How do we defeat evil like that?" Ava asked the priest.

Villalobos thought, staring at the house as it began to collapse. "We *don't* defeat evil like that," he said at last. "We fight it and keep fighting it. In the end, that's all we can do against evil. Fight it with all we have."

THE END

Dear reader,

We hope you enjoyed reading *The House On Blackstone Hill*. Please take a moment to leave a review, even if it's a short one. Your opinion is important to us.

Discover more books by Antonio Ricardo Scozze at https://www.nextchapter.pub/authors/antonio-ricardo-scozze

Want to know when one of our books is free or discounted? Join the newsletter at http://eepurl.com/bqqB3H

Best regards,

Antonio Ricardo Scozze and the Next Chapter Team

You might also like:
Ghost Song by Mark L'estrange

To read the first chapter for free, please head to:
https://www.nextchapter.pub/books/ghost-song

ABOUT THE AUTHOR

Extraordinarily little is known about Antonio Ricardo Scozze, the mysterious writer who appears to have knowledge of an esoteric world of horrors that is intertwined with our own. All that is known about him for certain is that he lives and writes in a small community called San Michele Vittoroso, and that all his writing is an attempt to pull back the veil on these hidden eldritch terrors.